Praise for A Little Harmless Submission:

Recommended Read from FALLEN ANGEL REVIEWS:
Once again, author Melissa Schroeder has written a sizzling story of BDSM, suspense and happily ever after. Rome, her dashing hero fights the demons of his past to be where he is today, but that doesn't stop him from thoroughly craving Maria, more than his next breath. Maria is an intelligent woman who keeps her vulnerabilities well hidden, an Alpha on the streets and a sub in the sheets. The witty repartee between these two is fun to read and as they build some amazing sexual tension, this reader felt less like a reader and more like a voyeuristic fly on the wall, watching the fetish fest unravel.
Bella, RR, Five Angels

Ms. Schroeder has written another great addition to the Harmless series and I can't wait for the next story.
Sabine, Manic Readers, 4.5 stars

Watching these two fall in love and deal with not only who they are now, but how the past shaped them, and what they want for the future was one of the best afternoon's I've spent reading.
The Book Reading Gals, A rating

TOP PICK FROM THE ROMANCE REVIEWS!!!!
A LITTLE HARMLESS SUBMISSION was just about perfect to me. It had the perfect mix of sexual tension, eroticism, suspense and cheekiness that I've come to associate with Melissa Schroeder's writing. I can't wait to see where the series will take me next!
Rho, The Romance Reviews, Five Stars

For a tough as nails Dom, hunting a sadistic serial killer is nothing compared to losing his heart.

Harmless #6

Rome Carino is hunting a predator. One who likes to hurt submissives, and the most popular BDSM club's patrons are being targeted. With each fresh kill he gets more brazen. Rome knows he just needs one little break, but before he can make headway, the FBI shows up. Worse, the uptight, buttoned-down Special Agent Maria Callahan suggests a plan that is dangerous, but worth it because it might just catch the killer. If Rome can keep his mind on the case and off the beautiful FBI agent, he'll be just fine.

Maria is still trying to step out of her legendary father's shadow and knows just how to do it. Luring the killer by posing as Rome's new sub seems like a good idea. That is, until undercover becomes real life and she finds herself tangled up with a man who amazes and scares her at the same time. Her growing attraction to the Honolulu Police Detective is a little too much to handle. Even knowing that, she can't help falling in love with the tough Dom and losing herself in the games they play in the bedroom.

Rome is overwhelmed by his need for Maria. He has never had a sub respond to him the way she does, and no matter what he does, he feels himself slipping off that cliff into love. As their relationship starts to unfold, he realizes that he will do anything to win her heart, to convince her to become his sub for a lifetime. But before he can do anything, the killer turns his attention on Rome and the one thing he holds dear: Maria.

WARNING: The following book contains: A Dom who thinks he can do no wrong, a new sub who is about to teach him he can, palm trees, a trip or two to Rough 'n Ready, a flirty Aussie Dom with questionable motives, old friends, and a new enemy. Yeah, it might be called Harmless, but you Addicts know it's anything but.

Dedication

To my Harmless Addicts. You kept the series going when most would have given up on it. Let's face it, people did. But you hung in there and helped me take this scary step. Thank you for your support and your threats of bodily harm. Know that this one, as all of them are, is especially for you.
Love,
Mel

Acknowledgements

I say over and over that no book is written without help. This time was definitely not the exception. When I made the decision to step out on my own and self-pub the Harmless books, I didn't do it without support.

As always, Les and my girls were there to support me, tell me I wasn't crazy, and to ignore the fact that I'm a temperamental DIVA.

Brandy Walker, what can I say that would do you justice? You keep me grounded and keep me from going crazy. You know I LOVE all the lists you make for me.

A special thank you to Joy Harris who was sitting in my room when I made the decision and reassured me that I had made the right one.

Kris Cook, although he is the brother I never wanted, has been one of my biggest cheerleaders.

And to the people behind the scenes:

Kendra Egert for her wonderful cover art.

Chloe Vale who whipped my arse into shape with the edits and handling the print formatting.

And of course, April Martinez for doing the digital formatting.

I could not have done this without your help. Thank you.

A Little Harmless Submission

Melissa Schroeder

Chapter One

Rome cursed when the rain started to pound the top of his car. It figured he would get a call for a dead girl and it would rain like this. That's the way his luck had been going the last few months. Only with hurricanes did they get this wet in Honolulu. What little forensic evidence they could have found was probably being washed away right now. He hoped that CID got there early enough to collect samples. He turned down Kuhio Street and headed to the scene. He had an itch at the base of his neck that told him this fourth girl in three months was connected to the other three. In all his life, he had never believed in coincidences, and he wasn't about to start. What that meant for Rough 'n Ready was not something he wanted to contemplate right now. He would deal with that later.

He parked his car and sighed. There was very little media on the islands, but they all seemed to show up at his crime scenes lately. A small group had gathered at the front of the alley. Lord only knew how they discovered the scene, but on Oahu, it was like one big family. Everyone knew everyone else, and there was just no way to stop people from finding out.

He stepped out of the vehicle, grabbing a hat before shutting the door. He turned up his jacket collar against the rain. Lord, it was cold. Rome had gone soft. For a kid who grew up in Seattle, this would be nothing. Now, after just a few years, seventy degree weather had him shivering.

He shook those thoughts away and made his way to the scene. Several reporters tried to get a comment from him, but he ignored them as he pushed his way through the crowd. He was thankful to see the CID officers already working the scene.

He glanced down and saw the girl. And, like the others before, he knew her.

A rookie cop ran up, excitement and fear in his voice when he spoke. "Her name is Lisa Fender. Here's her wallet."

Rome accepted it and was thankful the young officer seemed to be holding it together. "Who called it in?"

"Tourist. He's over there," he motioned with his head. "Name's Matt Young."

Rome followed the direction of the officer's nod and found a young man standing, his face expressionless as he watched the scene in front of him. Truthfully, from what Rome could tell, the witness wasn't really watching anything. He was staring into nothing, as if in a daze. Shock probably.

After thanking the kid, he headed over to the witness. "Mr. Young?"

For a moment, Young didn't say anything. Rome started worrying the kid had gone over the edge and might need medical care. But, in that next moment, Young shook himself and seemed to focus on Rome. "Huh?"

"I'm sorry to bother you, but I'm Detective Carino. I was wondering if you could tell me what you saw."

Mr. Young swallowed, his Adam's apple bobbing as he nodded. Damn, he was young. In that instant, Rome felt ten years older than his thirty-five years. There was a good chance Young wasn't even old enough to drink.

The kid wiped his mouth on the sleeve of his shirt. "I was walking down here. Got left at a club by my buddy."

"He left you at a bar? Why?"

He sighed. "He hooked up."

Rome nodded, understanding the timeless ritual of young men. Being left behind at a bar for a hot woman wasn't that bad of a thing. As he studied the man, Rome recognized the buzz cut.

Fuck. Rome wasn't in the mood to deal with the military. "What service?"

The kid's eyes widened. "I have n-no idea—"

"Cut the shit. You're military."

He swallowed again, then his shoulders sagged. "Yeah. Army."

"And let me guess, too young to be in the club you were in? Not to mention, it's off limits to military."

He swallowed again. "Yeah."

"I don't give a shit about that. What I care about is that woman lying dead on the ground."

The kid started breathing through his mouth, and Rome should have seen it coming. As it was, he barely missed getting the kid's vomit on him. Rome jumped back with a curse as the private emptied his stomach contents on the street.

"Fuck."

"You said a mouthful, Carino."

Rome turned and found his partner of just over a year walking up behind him. Jackson Daniels—who everyone called Jack Daniels just to piss him off—was officially his partner for the next three days. The paperwork was already filed, and Jack would be gone before the month was out.

"What are you doing here?" Rome asked.

He shrugged. "I got the call, too. Thought I would stop by."

His knowing look told Rome that his partner thought the same thing he did. "You can't finish out the investigation."

"Yeah, but I can take the rest of the kid's statement. Why don't you get over there with the body, talk to the geeks?"

Rome wanted to correct Jack's use of the name, but

decided to ignore it. Jack was the kind of cop that would use the science CID gave them, but hated it just the same. It was one of the things that had always been a bone of contention between the two of them. Thank God Jack wasn't Rome's responsibility anymore.

"Sure. I got up to the part where he and his other underage buddy parted ways because of a hot girl."

Jack shot him a grin. "Hey, it happens."

Rome chuckled as he turned and worked his way toward the scene. He could just imagine what it had been like for a woman to walk down the alley. Lights illuminated the dark corners now, but it would have been gloomy, dank…not to mention the smell of rotting food and booze. No one, whether woman or man, would walk down this alley without a purpose in mind. And definitely not alone.

The first person to notice him was Tim Takewodo, a first-rate detective with the CSI. He had been the lead on all the investigations so far, and having him there made Carino feel somewhat better.

"Hey, Carino. Glad to see that you got the call."

He nodded. "What ya have?"

Tim's smile faded. "Raped. Beaten, strangled. Coroner will have to give us the exact way she died. Panties are missing again."

He shot Tim a look.

"Yeah, I'm guessing manual strangulation like the others, and I'm sure he also used a scarf. I'm sure we will find the same fibers on her. I take it you know her?"

He looked back down at the young woman. He had seen her at Rough 'n Ready once or twice. "She looks a little familiar. I didn't recognize the name, but since I started working homicide, I haven't had as much time over at Rough 'n Ready."

It was a half-truth. Rome was avoiding his friends. He'd had to distance himself from his friends to make sure there were no questions later. He had learned a long time ago to never take anything for granted. He knew in his gut that Micah and Evan had nothing to do with this, but he needed that separation to make sure they didn't get tangled up in the investigation.

"They have a lot of new members, and with the new club opening on the other side of the island, they had to hire new people. She might be one of the newbies."

Tim sighed. "I'd lay odds. And this makes the fourth one."

Rome nodded, knowing it would prick the interest of the FBI. Dammit, he wasn't in the mood to deal with the feds. They would definitely come in and take over the case. "Find anything new?"

"Nope. Again, we can't be sure she was raped until there's a kit done."

Rome wanted to argue. Because the first three women had been regulars or worked at Rough 'n Ready, people thought they were into any kind of rough sex. Because a person was into BDSM didn't mean they would do something stupid. In fact, a lot of times, people in the life were smarter than most about that part of their life. Anyone with any sense wouldn't end up having sex in an alley of Kuhio Street. It was one of the rougher parts of Honolulu. Why leave the nice, warm environment of Rough 'n Ready and wander into a backstreet that would leave them vulnerable? Didn't make sense, but it was his job to make it make sense.

Rome glanced around. "Have you seen a car nearby that might be hers?"

"They did a search. Haven't found it, but that doesn't mean anything. You know if she was club hopping..."

She could have parked anywhere in the area. Tonight's weather aside, a person could probably bet on warm enough weather to make it from here to at least a bus stop.

"Thanks, Tim."

He turned and saw the coroner had arrived. The sooner

they got the poor woman out of here, the better. And then maybe they could find the bastard who did it.

Rome looked out over the crowd, wondering where the son of a bitch was hiding.

. . . . .

Maria Callahan pretended to be reading something on her computer as she waited. Still, she couldn't stop her toe from tapping. She wasn't very good at waiting. It was one of the few lessons her father had failed to teach her. It was hard to be patient when something that could make or break your career was being decided.

She knew this was The Dom. Maria grimaced. That name irritated her, but reporters thought it was catchy. Damn reporters were making it damned hard to catch him. These new killings in Hawaii were him. She could feel it to her bones. Besides that, she had done enough research to know it was him. Her plan could work, and for once, she had worked up the nerve to approach her supervisor about it. It was unorthodox, but it could work.

"Callahan!" Agent Smith bellowed. "Get in here."

It took every bit of her control not to jump and run.

Don't even let them see you sweat. Make them think they can't rattle you. Falling apart is for later.

Drawing in a deep breath, she slowly stood and walked to her supervisor's office. She shut the door.

His head was bent, showing her the bald spot none of them were allowed to mention. He had put on a few pounds in the last several years, but he was still in good shape. He signed a form then looked up at her. His face was expressionless. She still could not tell what her father's old partner was thinking. Then he smiled.

"It's a go. I talked to the HPD captain. He agreed we need to be there. He wants you working with his man."

She could barely pay attention for a few seconds. For the first time, she was going to head an investigation.

"Callahan." Smith sounded worried. She realized he had said her name several times. She gave herself a mental shake and focused her attention on her boss.

"Sorry," she said, then cleared her throat. "The detective? He's been checked out."

Smith nodded. "He's been on the island for the last eighteen months, except for one trip to Seattle for the weekend. Sister graduated from college. He didn't leave the area. So he's clean. Apparently he's pretty sharp, so try to play nice."

He said it sarcastically, and she tried not to wince. She didn't like the fact that she would be walking into a local department and taking over their investigation. It had to be done sometimes, but the behavior of some agents always upset the locals. For her plan to work, she would need their help, especially the lead detective.

"You'll take Masters."

She tried her best not to show her irritation, but failed. Smith knew her too well.

"You look just like your father when you get pissed."

She sighed. It was a problem working for a man who knew her family so well. Martin Smith had started at the FBI about the same time her father had. When her mother died, he had been the one there for them, the one to pick up the pieces. He and his wife were the closest thing she had to family. Which made it harder to conceal what she was thinking from him.

She settled down in the chair in front of his desk. "We don't get along. Other than his wife, I don't think he likes women. At least, he doesn't like me."

"You know why he's like that, why a lot of them are like that. Every single one of them thinks you got this job because of your father's legacy. But I can't send you without an agent who doesn't know how to run a case like this. He's only going to get you started, and then he'll come back. We want this low key, just like you said. If you need help, you're to contact the Honolulu office."

She nodded. "I understand. Doesn't mean I have to like it."

He chuckled. "I didn't ask you to like it. Just do your job."

~ People's opinions shouldn't matter, but they did. Not to her personally. More that it made her job harder to do when no one wanted to work with her. It wouldn't change until she solved a big case. It wasn't fair because she had a good reputation from her time in vice, but that didn't seem to matter. She pushed those morbid thoughts aside and stood to leave. It would do her no good to worry about people's perceptions. "If that's all?"

"Flight's at eight tomorrow morning from National. Make sure you make it on time."

She nodded and had her hand on the doorknob.

"Maria."

She looked back over her shoulder. "Yes?"

"This could be a huge step up for you, but please, be careful. This guy isn't just smart, he's fucking dangerous. We've never had a woman on the case before, and if he finds out, he might fixate on you."

She nodded again and slipped out the door. She wanted to dance down the hall, but she decided that would be unprofessional. Instead, she went to the bathroom and leaned up against the wall and let it sink in. She was going to Hawaii, and she was going to hunt The Dom killer. Panic settled in her chest first. In the five years she'd been with the FBI, she'd had to fight her way to the top. Sure, she had to work five times as hard as the other agents to prove herself, but there were always those whispers that Big John Callahan was the reason she got her start.

She pushed away from the wall and looked at herself in the mirror. She had his nose, and his mother had always claimed, his frown. But this time, she was going to prove that Big John Callahan's daughter was more than just the memory of a beloved agent.

. . . . .

"Carino," Captain Akada yelled down the hall. "Need you in my office right now."

Damn. Rome had almost escaped the building without having to talk to the captain. From the time Rome had returned from a call, Akada had been locked up in his office with some suits, which was fine by Rome. Three days after finding Lisa and they had nothing more than they did before. Hell, they almost had less than with the other three killings. The bastard was getting better. Worse, Rome knew the killer was getting more infatuated with his work.

He reached the door and discovered it open. He slipped in and found three people in the room. One was, of course, the captain, the other were two dark suited, very unhappy looking people. Feds.

The man was typical of the species. Dark suit, blank expression. He looked like the kind of guy who would sell his mother to the highest bidder to gain a promotion. Short brown hair, brown eyes, and a frown. Typical. The woman, not much different, but there was something vaguely familiar about her. The suit showed nothing of her body. Her dark hair was pulled back into a tight bun at the base of her neck. When she looked in his direction, he felt like he'd been punched in the gut. He hadn't expected the luminous blue eyes or the full, pouty lips. Her skin was flawless.

"Shut the door, Carino."

He shook himself out of his stupor and did as ordered. Since the other two chairs were occupied by the feds, he leaned against the wall.

"This is Brice Masters and Maria Callahan of the FBI."

He nodded in their direction. "What does the FBI from the mainland want with Honolulu PD?"

The woman's eyes widened, but if he hadn't been watching, he wouldn't have seen it. This one was used to hiding her feelings, but what fed wasn't trained to do that? Still, there was something ice cold about her behavior, something that bothered him on a level he couldn't understand. Possibly because he couldn't read her emotions, which left him on the outside.

"They've been chasing a serial killer. The Dom. They think he might be our guy."

Of course he had heard the name. It had been splashed on every headline for the last year. He wanted to argue with them, but he knew it would be useless. When the FBI sunk their teeth into an investigation, they didn't let go until they chomped off a huge piece.

Despite that, there was a good chance this was their guy. Without any DNA, he hadn't been able to make any kind of match. Still, he knew from the crime scenes, this wasn't an amateur. This was someone who was very good at what he was doing. This one had been killing for a while.

Still, he refused to let them know what he thought. "What makes you think that?"

Masters smiled and opened his mouth, but the woman beat him to answering.

"Let me make some assumptions about your man. He picks up women at BDSM clubs. Or singles them out. No one really knows how he finds them, but they all go to the same club. Then, he beats them, sometimes tortures them, rapes them, and in the end, strangles them with a combo of a scarf and then finally manual strangulation. Their panties are missing, also. Did I get it right?"

So close it made him twitch. "A bit."

The smile she offered him didn't reach her blue eyes and was as cold as the top of Mauna Loa. "Really? I have a feeling I was spot on."

10

He hated her cockiness. Besides the fact that she was correct, he didn't like the premonition that was winding its way through his brain at the moment. He glanced at the captain. "Are they taking over the case?"

Akada shook his head. "No. Not officially."

He allowed for a beat of silence to go by. "In what capacity?"

"Agent Callahan, would you like to explain?"

From the look on her face, she didn't want to, but she straightened her shoulders. When she turned all her attention in his direction, he felt like he had been hit by a bolt of lightning. His body reacted without him being able to control it. She had looked at him before, but now she was concentrating on him only. Her attention had his blood heating. Her eyes were so large, so luminous, they were at odds with her clothing. There was nothing staid about the dark blue gaze she trained on him. Even now, he couldn't seem to concentrate on what she was saying. His mind had melted the moment she'd looked directly at him. What the hell was wrong with him? It took all his power to get his head wrapped around the idea that he should be paying attention to her.

"We've gotten close to our man a few times. Of course, we don't go in right away because we usually wait for a few deaths before we try to take over. Our problem is that every time we show up on the scene, our man disappears into thin air. Well, when the former agents showed up."

The look she got from the other agent told her he wasn't happy she relayed that bit of info. She ignored him. Or pretended to. There was a slight wince after she realized what she said. Revealing the FBI was fucking things up wasn't always the smartest thing to do. They liked to pretend they were invincible.

From Rome's study, Masters was older than Callahan. Probably sent to supervise, and that wouldn't go over well with a go-getter like Callahan. Masters, for his part, didn't look happy about being there.

"So, you move in to investigate, he vanishes?" he asked, already getting a sour feeling in his stomach.

She nodded once. The gesture was familiar. There had been an agent, one of the first profilers who hunted serial killers. John Callahan. The eyes should have told him. Almost luminous blue, just like her father's.

"That can mean only one thing."

Yeah, and Rome didn't like it one bit. "He's one of you or one of us. Or someone connected to us. Someone with access to this kind of info."

Her eyebrows arched in surprise, and Rome tried not to get pissed. He failed. The fact that she thought he wasn't smart enough to figure that out irritated him. He expected it, had dealt with it before, but for some reason it made him mad.

She moved her hands on her lap. He noticed that she didn't wear any rings, and for some odd reason, he was relieved by that. If he hadn't been that intrigued by that, he wouldn't have noticed the way her thumb tapped her leg. The movement was so slight, he would have missed it if he hadn't been paying attention. She was nervous.

"If we come in here and take over, he'll know. He has some kind of connection, whether it's through him or someone he's close to, someone he knows. Since I'm new to the case, he won't know me, won't pick up on me being here for it. But we can't let anyone know I'm with the FBI."

He studied the two of them and shook his head. "Then you better do something about the way you're dressed. Did anyone see you come in?"

She glanced at Masters then down at her own suit. When she looked up, she grimaced. "Dammit, you're probably right."

He shouldn't want to help Callahan, but something in him wanted to make sure she stayed. "We'll fix it. We can say that there was an old case from Seattle when I worked homicide there. Then you two need to assimilate."

"What does that mean?" Masters asked, but his partner was smarter.

She sighed. Rome could barely hear it, but he picked up on her irritation. "Look around, Masters. People don't wear suits here. I should have thought of it, but we came straight from the airport."

At least she was smart enough not to get pissed at him for pointing it out. Which in his book made her smarter than the average agent. "Where are you staying?"

She didn't even allow her partner to speak. The older agent might have been sent to babysit Callahan, but she definitely saw herself in charge. "Right now, the Hilton Hawaiian Village. But we're looking for something more permanent."

Masters made a face. It was easy to see the agent didn't want to be here. Of course, it was probably more to do with who he was with. No one, not even Rome, would want to come to Hawaii with a woman who didn't know how to have fun.

"Okay. I'll meet you for drinks in the lounge right by the big pool at the Hilton."

She said nothing for a second but studied him as if he were a bug of some sort. Then, she nodded. "Time?"

"Seven."

She sighed. "Okay. Let's go, Masters."

Both of them stood, and Rome couldn't help but admire her height. He glanced at her shoes and saw that she wore low heels. She was as tall as Masters. The agents walked out the door, and it shut with an almost silent snick.

For a moment, the captain said nothing. Then he chuckled. "That was very friendly of you, Carino."

He watched Callahan and Masters walk through the squad room until they disappeared through the door. Rome shot a smile over his shoulder at his boss. "Considering who her father is, I figured I'd play nice."

"Was. Big John died about eighteen months ago. Did you know him?"

He nodded, thinking of the giant man he'd heard talk. "Went to a few of his lectures years ago when I was stationed in the DC area."

"Make sure you continue to make nice. The FBI might want to take this over, but I want to make sure that when we catch this son of a bitch, Honolulu PD gets some credit."

Rome offered his boss an angelic smile. "I promise to be a good boy."

"I didn't tell them your connection to the club, but I think you better tell her. She's pretty sharp, and if you aren't careful, you'll find yourself off the case."

He nodded and headed out the door. No matter what, he was on the case until he caught the bastard. And no one, not the FBI or the HPD, would tell him differently.

Chapter Two

Maria was nervous. Her entire body sizzled with energy that was draining her concentration. She had faced down felons that would scare the bejesus out of most grown men, but none of them made her feel as nervous as Detective Carino. It was embarrassing to admit that Carino made her palms sweat.

It wasn't uncommon for her to be edgy at work. She had never really fit in at the FBI, and she knew she never would. Every little bit of the job made her feel out of place. She hated the adrenaline rush before a raid, and she really hated questioning suspects. Still, Carino made her off her game. And not in the way that most adversaries did. She couldn't get the cool, quiet detective out of her head. Good lord, she didn't even know the man, and he had her almost drooling. There was something about the way he moved, all quiet control…It made her shiver.

She pulled in a deep breath and looked out over the pool area. She needed to get her reaction to him under control. Acting this way could end up being embarrassing for her. Besides that, she could lose the edge she had over him right now. She knew he understood if he didn't play nice, he could lose any hopes of solving the case. If she wanted to be a complete ass, she could take over the investigation. But she didn't want to do that. She wanted his help. No, she needed

it. Not that she would let him know how much she needed
him. That would be a mistake with a man like Rome Carino.

With considerable effort, she sipped on her white wine.
As the cool liquid slid down her throat, she thought how she
would prefer a swift shot of whiskey. She ordered herself to
calm down, and she took another drink. It was her idea to
work together. It was a great plan. All of it, including the part
she didn't tell them about, was solid. Now that she was here
in Hawaii, she wanted to go run and hide. What the hell had
she been thinking?

You weren't thinking, little girl.

Maria shook her head, trying to push that thought aside,
but she knew it was no use. How many times did she hear
that from her father? More than a thousand, she was sure. He
would have approved of her plan. It was good, solid, and
coming in under the radar was the best way to do it. He
definitely would not be happy with her reaction to Detective
Carino.

"Daydreaming, Agent Callahan?"

She started at the deep, resonate voice that came from
beside her. Drawing in a deep breath, she tried to prepare
herself before looking at him. She just hoped she wouldn't
swallow her tongue. He was standing so close, she was
amazed she hadn't heard him walk up.

There was no doubt about it. The man was a god. She
knew for a fact there wasn't a heterosexual woman alive who
would argue with her. He was tall, so tall, that she had to
look up at him. Since she was five foot eleven in her stocking
feet, that didn't happen that often. He wasn't just tall, but he
also had those movie star looks. A strong jaw, swarthy skin,
and long, long eye lashes were enough to attract just about
any woman. Add in the hazel eyes that seemed greener now
that he was in the natural sunlight and he was near perfection.
His dark hair was military short, but she could tell it was
thick and probably very well given to curl. Full sensual lips
completed the package, and she had to fight the urge to lick

her own. He would be considered pretty if he hadn't had his nose broken more than once.

"Agent Callahan?"

"Yes." Great. Yeah, really a way to impress the local law. She was staring at him like she was a fifteen-year-old with a crush. "Sorry. I've been up for about forty hours or so."

One of his eyebrows rose. "I didn't know you just got here."

She tried to tell herself not to get irritated, but she hated repeating herself. Especially when she was sure he did remember what she'd said earlier. Power plays were one thing she despised. "As I said at the station, we'd come straight from the airport. It's the reason we were in our suits. You remember that, right?"

His smile told her he did. "And you look much more relaxed now."

She looked down at her outfit, knowing it probably still looked too formal for Hawaii. The short sleeved red shirt and khaki shorts weren't as flashy as a lot of the other tourists' clothes, but it was the only thing she could think of wearing. Most of her other clothes were too formal, and she knew that she couldn't wear her workout clothes to their meeting.

He paused, his hands still in his pockets. "You want to wait to talk about this?"

She shook her head. "I'm anxious to get to everything that isn't in the report."

He looked around the bar. "I think we need to go somewhere more private. Is Masters in the room?"

"He's in his room. I've got my own."

He nodded and waited. Again, she liked the fact that he seemed to take his time to talk. So many men said the first thing that came to their mind. "Why don't we take a walk on the beach?"

She nodded, setting down her drink. He waited for her to step in front of him. An odd feeling. She spent so much time with men who treated her as another one of them, she always

17

found it strange when men held chairs or doors for her. The moment he touched her back, she had to fight a shiver. He was warm, and—she thought—so was she. But the moment he touched her, heat and craving rolled through her.

When they reached the sidewalk, she waited for him to draw even with her, and then they started to walk.

"You have very nice legs, Agent Callahan." The amusement in his voice didn't bother her as much as she thought he might like it to. She knew that local police officers had to take a few swings at them.

"I hate suits, especially in humid weather."

"Then why wear them?"

She shrugged and looked out over the beach. "It's expected."

She sensed, rather than saw him nod.

"I met your father once."

That took her by surprise. Maria didn't know why because she should have been used to people knowing her father, especially in law enforcement. He had been a celebrity of sorts, regularly interviewed on television. She glanced at Rome, but he was looking ahead of them.

"Really?"

He nodded. "I was stationed in the DC area, and he did a few lectures about different procedures."

"He was good at that." She could hear the pride in her own voice. Even if he had driven her crazy reciting his rules and regs while she was growing up, Maria knew her father had been a good lecturer. Hell, he had been good at anything he tried. "I think it was why he was so good at criminal profiling. He always said that following the rules would lead you to the man."

They walked for a few more steps, and then she asked, "You were in the military?"

He glanced at her. "I would have thought you read my entire file."

"I didn't have time. I read most of it, but I spent a lot of the trip going over each of your cases and comparing them to the others. What service?

"Marines."

Like her father. "You weren't in long enough to make it a career?"

He shook his head. "No. My father got sick, and I needed to get back to Seattle."

She waited, but he didn't continue. She knew he'd been a cop for a few years in Seattle, but not much else other than the proof he wasn't connected to the case and that he was a member of the biggest BDSM club on the island. They walked on a few steps, the crashing of the surf and the busy walkway the only sounds she heard.

"Okay, so you want to talk about the case?" she asked.

"Not really."

They continued to walk in silence for a while, and he turned into the lobby area and then headed toward the Tapa Tower where she was staying.

"How did you know where I was staying?"

"With your job, they weren't going to spring for the Ali'I Tower. And the Tapa Tower is the one people usually get at the last minute."

She nodded as they walked to the elevators. The moment they stepped onto the car, a family of Japanese tourist rushed aboard. She was forced to step closer to Carino. She could feel the heat of him warm her arm. The spicy scent had nothing to do with cologne and everything to do with the man. Neither of them said a word on the ride. Once they stepped off the elevator, he followed her silently to her room. By the time they were in her room, she had her mind back on the case, and apparently he did too.

"So, you want to tell me what you know?"

She nodded. "Not much. I take it from what I read you had no samples for DNA?"

"No."

"Which a few years ago would have meant he was

involved with the police in some way. But now, with all the information out there, everyone knows that."

He frowned. "Still, the crime scenes are too clean."

She sighed and settled on her bed. "I know. I saw it right off."

He crossed his arms and frowned. "There's nothing in the reports I could find."

She was tired, so tired, and right now, the first rush of adrenaline after seeing Rome was starting to fade. "I wasn't primary on it, as I said. And I couldn't really say anything."

A look of understanding moved over his face. "So the first agent fucked up the investigation."

She shrugged. "Not really. His wife served him with divorce papers about halfway through the investigation."

He opened his mouth, and she held up her hand to forestall any comments.

"I agree, he should have removed himself from the case. I would have, and I am pretty sure you would have."

"You can be damned sure I wouldn't. I just wouldn't let it interfere."

Okay, so he was sort of like the other men she knew. They all thought they were ten feet tall and bullet proof. Like her father up until the bitter end.

"It started in Phoenix at a club called The Velvet Whip."

"I thought it was at The Dungeon in Seattle?"

She shook her head. "Those were the first reported incidents, but the MO of the killings in Phoenix were a lot like the others. In fact, just about down to a T, but he did make a few alterations. They tend to do that."

He nodded and continued to watch her. She had a feeling she was being weighed and measured on a professional level. She was used to it from everyone she worked with. For some reason, though, his contemplation irked her.

"Why don't we go back to my place? I think we have a lot to talk about, and I haven't had anything to eat."

She glanced at him out of the corner of her eye. Normally

she would say no. She didn't feel like going. It had been a long trip over, and she was on hour forty-something of being awake. She knew the drill, too. Most of the time, something like this was a prelude to him trying to get her in bed. But she had a feeling with Carino, it wouldn't be a problem. This was a man who never mixed business and pleasure. Besides, the one little tidbit she did know about him was that he was a practicing Dom. Since no one would ever call her a submissive woman, it was a pretty sure bet he wouldn't be interested in her. Still, it would probably get them off to a good start of working together. If she could control her attraction and not slobber on him, she would be good to go.

"Sure, why not?"

. . . . .

Rome tried to keep his head straight as he turned the car onto his street. He'd suggested going to his house because seeing her on that hotel bed had been a little too much temptation. But now, he felt an odd sort of thrill that he would see her in his house. He was having a really hard time keeping himself on the straight and narrow, and it made no sense. She wasn't his type of woman. Or, he thought she wasn't. It had nothing to do with her looks. She was like most women in her career field. Almost every one of them dressed like they thought a man would dress if he were a woman. Callahan was no different. But, he would bet there was a tight, athletic body beneath the ugly suit. Not to mention the legs that seemed to go on forever. She didn't wear much makeup, but, truthfully, she didn't really need it. Amazing skin, sculpted cheekbones, and those electric blue eyes. There was enough there to make a man want to look beneath that tough surface.

For some reason, though, his body didn't care that she probably wasn't a sub. Every time he was around her, there

21

was a low-level hum that filtered through his blood. It was enough to drive a man crazy. He sighed, trying to keep his mind on the objective. He wanted this bastard and so did Callahan. Thinking about a woman who didn't want him would only cause problems. Besides, Rome didn't get involved with female partners. Not after what happened in Seattle.

Again, she pulled him out of his thoughts. "I'm sorry for butting into the investigation."

God, that voice was going to drive him crazy. It was so sultry, seductive. It was making his body ache to hear her moan. It was totally at odds with the woman she presented to the world.

"First, be truthful. You probably had to fight tooth and nail to get over here. They pulled the case from someone else, but they gave it to a younger agent, someone with no background in the field."

"Except she was trained by the best serial killer hunter who ever lived."

He heard the pride in her voice, just as he had earlier. There were definitely some issues there, but she had been very proud of her father's work. "To get back to your earlier comment. I have no problem with it, especially the way we are going to handle this. We need the capabilities of the FBI."

He sensed her nod as he turned into his carport. He turned off the car and then noticed she was staring at him.

"What?"

She shook her head and said nothing as she slipped out of the car. He followed suit, and then lead the way to the front door. After unlocking the door, they both stepped into the foyer, and he was glad that he'd hired maid service to come in once a month. And thanked God it was the day after a visit.

He led her into the living room, and after they settled down, he said, "Okay. Go."

She nodded. "Our guy is probably between thirty and forty-five, and he likes dark-headed women usually. Athletic build, white most of the time, although there have been a few Hispanic women in his pickings."

He nodded, knowing all of this. He had been following the case for months since they'd found Samantha Brown.

"So he kills a number of women, then the FBI descends, he disappears."

She hesitated. "Before the press even knows we're there."

That tidbit sent a slice of ice racing through his blood.

"Before the press catches wind, the killings stop?"

She nodded. "They were in Atlanta for three weeks before the press found out."

Hell, this was worse than he thought. If the press had known first, there was a good chance there might be someone in their ranks who had done this. But if the press hadn't been sniffing around, that really did narrow it down to law enforcement and people directly connected to them.

"I see from your expression you understand the implications."

His gut was churning just thinking about it. "This is someone who travels. Could he be FBI?"

He expected her to get irritated, but she just nodded again. "Yeah, that's one of my worries."

"I'm surprised that I didn't piss you off."

She offered him a wry smile. "It takes a lot to piss me off mainly because I work for the federal government in a career field filled with men. Besides, my father said never rule anyone out. That mistake has cost too many lives in the past."

"So we need to start going through a database of people in the FBI."

"Done. There weren't many names on the list that fit the criteria.."

He studied her for a moment. "Are you taking a risk doing this?"

"I don't know what you mean."

"I would think that putting yourself in this situation would put you out there to be attacked if you fail."

She shrugged. "People are always waiting for me to fail." She said it as if it were a fact. "Because you're a woman?"

Chuckling, she said, "No. Actually it's because I'm Big John Callahan's daughter. I have a lot to prove. I can send you that list if you can give me your email."

She was already pulling out her phone when he asked, "Why don't we have something to eat?"

The moment he said it, he wanted to call back the words. He meant to stop on the way, just pick up something fast. But he'd been so preoccupied with Callahan and what he would like to do to her, he'd forgotten. Shit, he didn't even know if he had something to feed her. He opened his mouth to tell her to forget it. But a second later, she looked up, surprise lighting her eyes. That look alone had his hands itching. There was something about the expression that had him reassessing his original thoughts on her preferences. A hint of vulnerability along with interest in her gaze made him rethink everything. And he could tell she was trying to decide what to do.

"Sure."

A strange sense of relief swept through him. Damn, he was acting like some kind of fifth grader with a crush on his teacher. "I'll go see what I have on hand."

"Oh, you don't have to go to any trouble."

She gave him an out. He didn't have to follow through on his offer, but strangely, he didn't want that out. He wanted to spend more time with her. Rome just had to figure out if it was because of her or the case.

"No worries."

. . . . .

Maria really didn't know what to think of her new partner, for lack of a better word. She knew a lot of men. It was hard not to in her field. Since her mother had died when Maria was twelve, she'd been raised by her father. For the better part of the last fifteen years, she had actually spent more time with men than with women. She didn't think any of the men she knew intrigued her more than the man presently sitting across the table from her. He had thrown together a quick meal of grilled shrimp and vegetables, served it on what he called the lanai, and while they talked of the case, he never tried to take the lead. From what she knew in his files, she had expected him to be different. Very different.

"So you have Masters checking out these guys?"

She nodded as she took a sip of white wine, another shock. Most of the men she worked with had a great selection of beer in their houses, but Rome seemed to be a bit of a connoisseur of wines. And he'd had one of her favorites.

"He's going to do some digging, then leave."

His eyebrows rose. "Whose call was that?"

"Mine. If I'd had my way, he wouldn't be here at all. But the boss wanted to be sure I had a seasoned agent with me. And dragging him all this way and letting him leave actually got me brownie points with Masters." In fact, the expectant father had been embarrassingly thankful when she'd told him.

"Why didn't you want him here?"

"He wasn't needed. And his wife is about to give birth. It's their first, and it's been a difficult pregnancy. I can understand that he would want to be there with her."

Rome shrugged. "Then why did you bring him?"

She sighed. "My supervisor wanted me to have backup in case…"

"Let me guess? He expected me to buck you?"

"That, and there are standards, and people gossip. This way he covers his ass."

"You were surprised when I agreed to help."

She laughed. "You really have no choice but to let me butt in. I appreciate it, and I understand why departments get so pissed. Hell, the way we've been going into cities and taking over has led to some really bad relations over this case. I do know that they almost let a murderer get away because they lumped one woman's murder in with The Dom. Turned out it was just her ex."

"You're sure this is the same guy?"

"Letting you handle the investigation, we can find out. If the others had come in, there was a good chance they would have taken over. Plus, this is an ideal place to corner the bastard."

He studied her for a second or two. "Explain."

"On the mainland, it's harder to keep up with who has come in and out of a city. Here, it will be easier to find out who was here and on what dates. Being that it is an island allows us to study a very small list of people. Well, a smaller list of people."

"That makes sense. So what is this plan you have? You're going to have me investigate, and you're going to do what?"

She could tell from his skeptical tone that he didn't trust her. Which made him a smart man.

"You're a member of the club."

He studied her for a second then nodded. Brownie points to the detective for not lying about that. "It's not a big secret. But I don't have anything to do with this."

She waved that away. "You've never been to the other clubs. Plus, you don't fit the profile, and the only other city you were in was Seattle. Of course, that wasn't during the killings there."

Again, he studied her. She knew she was being weighed, tested in some way again. Her father had often looked at everyone that way—including her.

"So what's your role in this? Other than resources, what

26

are you going to offer me?"

She drew in a deep breath and decided it was time to bite the bullet. Waiting was only going to prolong the issue, and she wanted to start right away.

"I'm going to be bait."

Chapter Three

Shock held Rome immobile for a few seconds. His brain just refused to function. He heard the words, but they just didn't seem to make sense. In that next instant, anger blazed through his blood.

"No fucking way." He ground out the words, more than a little surprised by the vehemence in his tone. Even to his own ears, he sounded territorial.

She frowned at him. He didn't know if it was his language or his reaction that she objected to. He didn't really care.

She straightened her shoulders. "I wasn't asking." Her voice had turned a little bit prissy, and dammit, he even found that attractive. There was something definitely wrong with him.

"I said no."

"I didn't really ask." Her tone told him that she wasn't happy with him. Hell, he wasn't happy with himself. It wasn't that it was a stupid idea. Part of him realized it was probably a good plan. But the thought of her strutting through Rough 'n Ready had his blood running cold. Or hot, thinking of what he would do to the first man who approached her. He pushed aside the oddly possessive feelings and put his mind back on track.

"There are a ton of reasons you shouldn't do this."

Her brow furrowed. "Can you think of one reason I shouldn't?"

"First, it's too dangerous."

She rolled her eyes and took a sip of her wine. "Yes, of course. I can't handle myself. I'm only a trained FBI agent. Heck, I traveled with my father from the time I was thirteen. I know how to handle myself."

For a second, he was sidetracked by her comment. "You went with your father on jobs?"

She shrugged. "After my mother was…after she died, we had little to no family to take care of me. When my father made noises about quitting, his supervisor made sure I could go along with him if he got called out."

Being considered one of the pioneers of criminal profiling, John Callahan could probably have asked for just about anything and gotten it. But what kind of man dragged a thirteen-year-old with him while hunting down the most disgusting scum of the universe? And just what the hell did it do to the woman sitting in front of him?

"Carino."

He shook himself out of his stupor. "Doesn't matter. I don't think it will work."

She cocked her head to the side and studied him again. A strand of hair had escaped the tight bun. It was long, well past her shoulders, and he started to wonder how long it was. Did it trail all the way down her back so that he could spread it out over his sheets? He could just imagine threading his fingers through it as she took his cock deep inside her mouth.

"Why?" she asked.

He shifted in his seat, trying to ease the erection the image had created. "Why what?"

She sighed. "Why don't you think it would work? It's a good plan. With your help, it could very well catch the killer."

"You're not submissive."

The smile she offered him told Rome she thought he had

just praised her. "Thanks."

"That wasn't a compliment. That was an observation."

But now that he said it, he wondered. In her job, she had to be a ballbuster or people would walk all over her. He knew through his training that people in their real lives were many times vastly different than what they needed in the bedroom. He knew a few cops who were Doms, but he also knew a florist from Mokuleia who was the toughest Dominatrix he'd ever known. In her real life, she generally struck people as a very soft-spoken woman, but he knew she was sought after at the club. Most people, those who knew nothing of the life, would consider Callahan and her job and assume she was a Dominatrix. But there were little tells that hinted that she might like to play the submissive. And for some reason, an image of her popped into his head. She was on his bed, hands tied behind her back, and he was spanking her ass red. He had to bite back a groan as he tried to cover up his reaction and get rid of the idea. Try as he might, he couldn't get it out of his head.

"It's a role. I've done undercover before." She shrugged. "And I have your help. I understand you have *quite* the reputation."

The idea that she saw him as some stepping-stone was irritating. And worse, he hated that she had something in her file on him. Like he was part of the case. She reached for the bottle of wine, but he grabbed it away and set it beside his plate.

"I think you've had enough of that."

She shrugged. "If you say so."

"I do."

Her eyebrows lifted at his tone, but he couldn't help it. His Dom wanted out, and he wanted her under his control.

"What did your supervisor say?" he asked.

"Do you do everything by the book?"

"That answers my question. So he didn't approve of it."

She looked out over his small lawn. "I never said

anything."

Now she sounded a little petulant, and normally, he would have been confused by the change in her. But she was tired, and she'd had two glasses of wine. He had a feeling Callahan wasn't a heavy drinker.

The idea of having her in the club, playing a role to capture a killer…it just didn't sit right with him. It was odd because he'd worked undercover in Seattle PD and never had a problem with a woman putting herself in danger. If she were trained, he treated her as an equal. But he couldn't take that chance again.

"So you've gone rogue?"

She snorted. "Hardly. I spent a lot of time thinking of this. I am putting myself out there to attract the killer. I might not even do that. But I could find things out that you might not be able to."

"Are you saying you're a better investigator than me?"

"No. But people know you're a cop. Without knowing it, they hold back. Maybe not on purpose, but just a reflex."

"Just because they're members doesn't mean they're hiding anything."

"I don't mean that. But no matter how good the person is, there is always a knee-jerk reaction. You come along, they shut up."

"And if you are thought to be involved with me, that would cause problems."

She nodded. "Could, but I'm willing to take that chance."

"And everyone on the island, especially this killer, knows I'm handling the case. You have the physical attributes he likes. It will definitely make you a target."

"You'll be there. I read your file. You've done undercover work before."

"With backup. I've done this a lot, but we always had backup. Since you don't have permission to do this—and neither do I—we won't be able to have backup. No wires, no surveillance, what are we going to gain from this?"

31

"First, it is more to gain information that might help us narrow down the field. When people freeze up, they forget those little details. If they think I'm one of them, not connected to the police except for you, they might remember something. We have to connect these women outside the club beyond that they just knew each other. With the backup, I think Micah Ross can help us there," she said, naming one of the owners of the club. "He used to bounty hunt. I figured we would get their approval anyway."

Before he could argue more, his front doorbell rang. He wasn't expecting anyone, so he figured it was someone who was lost.

"I'll be right back."

She said nothing as he walked away. When he opened the door, he found Micah himself standing on the stoop, along with his wife, Dee.

"I hope you have a moment to talk," Micah said.

Dee rolled her eyes. "What Micah means is he hopes you aren't busy."

"I'm actually working."

Dee looked down at his bare feet then smiled up at him. "Really?"

He needed to get them away. He knew that if Callahan knew they were here, she would definitely approach Micah about her plan. And while he counted Micah as a friend, he would do anything to protect Dee and the women at that club. It probably wouldn't take much for him to be persuaded.

"Rome, are you going to invite us in?"

"Yeah, Rome, are you going to invite them in?" Maria asked from behind him.

He could feel his lip curling into a snarl, but he suppressed the urge to growl. Barely. Dee looked around him, her intelligent eyes taking in the situation, her gaze moving down Callahan's impressive length to her bare feet. When she looked up at Rome, she didn't even try to disguise her interest. He gritted his teeth. There was no way around it now.

"Yeah, sure, come on in."

. . . . .

By the time they were all seated on the lanai, Maria was fuming. Dammit, she had thought more of Rome Carino. She'd read his file, had seen he had no problem working with women. There was a little something about a woman in Seattle, but other than one personal involvement, there was nothing else. In fact, his last captain in Seattle had been a woman who gave him glowing marks. She hadn't thought he would go all Neanderthal on her.

"So there's a connection to the Dom murders?" Micah asked.

She turned her attention to the co-owner of Rough 'n Ready. She had read his file and had seen his picture, but it was hard not to be impressed with the man sitting across the table. He was tall, strong, exactly what you would think a sexy Native American male would look like. And a woman would have to be crazy to be able to resist all that long, dark, silky hair.

"We think there is. Since he leaves no DNA, it's hard to say, but everything points to the fact that he's the same guy. It is downright freaky the way he doesn't leave any evidence."

"There was a mistake with that one guy in Dallas, right?" Dee Ross, Micah's wife asked.

Maria turned her attention to the woman who seemed to have tamed Micah Ross. She wasn't a big woman, kind of petite, but she packed a punch. Long, straight blonde hair, blue eyes, and a quirky little smile that told Maria that Dee Ross wasn't anyone's fool. Maria could feel Rome's study. "Yes. That's why I could convince my supervisor that we shouldn't even let the local law enforcement know about us being here."

"But you told us," Dee said.

"Yes, I need your cooperation. You own the club, and if we're going to be running around there, you should know about it."

"No." Rome's hard denial caused all three of them to look at him. "I said no. I mean it."

Micah studied them for a second or two. "You want to do some kind of sting at my club?"

She nodded even as she could feel Rome's anger building. She had the training, and he was just being an ass about it. "I think it would work if I went undercover as a sub. I fit the build of the women. Plus, if the detective who is in charge is interested in me, it would probably gain his interest."

"They're all subs, so it makes sense you'd go in as one," Micah said.

"And you'll want to dress the part. I take it you don't have a lot of clothes that would fit the bill?" Dee asked.

She smiled, excitement sizzling along her blood. Ross' agreement would make it much easier. "No. I can go shopping."

"I can take you. May will need to know also," Dee offered.

She opened her mouth to agree, but Rome stood and said, "There is no fucking way I'm doing this. I'll call DC and report you if you think to do it on your own."

With that, he stomped off, leaving the three of them staring after him. She glanced at Micah and Dee and realized this wasn't regular behavior from the strange looks on their faces. "I guess I should go talk to him."

Micah shook his head. "No, you stay. I'll talk to him." He brushed his mouth over Dee's cheek then left in search of their irritated host.

Dee looked at her. "I guess you know about my family?"

"That your father was organized crime, and both he and

your brother tried to have you killed."

"Thank God." Dee sighed, the sound filled with relief. "I hate explaining that to people. So, how you liking Hawaii so far?"

. . . . .

"Not acting normal there, bruddah," Micah said from behind Rome.

Rome continued to rinse the plate off and said nothing.

"If this is because of what happened back in Seattle, this is totally different. Your partner there was dirty. She put herself in that situation."

He rolled his shoulders. "It isn't because of that."

It would be easier if it was because of Renee and her duplicity. Rome feared it was much worse.

"Worried about getting in trouble over this?"

He turned off the water and faced Micah. He hadn't made a lot of friends since moving to Hawaii. It was his way of making sure to keep his nose clean and his reputation above reproach. After getting to know May and Evan, he'd been pulled into a friendship of sorts with the little group of friends that included Micah and Dee. Then, after a few months, he'd been offered a free membership at Rough 'n Ready. He started getting invited to picnics, weddings…hell, he was like a member of their family now.

"No. Actually, I think it might work." That was the problem. If her father had trained her, she would do anything to get her man. Anything that could end up getting that pretty neck of hers wrung.

"Then why?"

"First, she's not a sub. She knows nothing of the life."

Micah crossed his arms over his chest and studied him. "You asked?"

"No."

35

His friend shrugged. "It's a role. She's done undercover before according to her, right?"

He shoved his hand through his hair and tried his best to come up with a reason. He was afraid he knew the real answer, and he wasn't going to admit that to Micah. "This is very dangerous. This guy…you haven't seen what I have, Micah. The man is a sadistic fuck. And she's saying she wants to put herself out there and wave her arms around and yell 'come get me.'"

Micah leaned a hip against the counter and studied him for a moment. "She's trained. She knows what she's doing. I have a feeling that she knows exactly what she's getting into."

"Yeah. Big John Callahan's daughter would know."

Micah frowned. "Why does that name sound familiar?"

"He's been profiled a lot. He hunted serial killers. He wrote a lot of books."

Micah's eyes widened. "Ah, yeah. I saw something on one of those 'true life' shows one time about him. He's done a lot of consulting. She does know what she's doing, I bet. Besides, bra, I think you're wrong about the submissive thing."

That caught his attention. Micah was good at listening to his gut. Being a former bounty hunter, his friend was good at reading people. "Yeah, and why do you say that?"

Micah shrugged. "I just have a feeling. Of course, I had the same feeling about Dee when everyone thought I was insane."

Just hearing Micah say it had Rome's curiosity peaked. He could just imagine her now, strapped down, her ass red from a spanking.

"Ah, I thought so."

He felt the heat of blush in his face. Jesus, he was blushing. He hadn't done that since he was a teenager. Rome pretended to be very interested in the dishes. "What?"

"You're attracted to her. That's why you don't want to do

this." Micah held up his hand. "Don't even deny it."

He rinsed off a dish. "She's an attractive woman."

Micah nodded. "She could be, but she tries her best not to be. If she's going to succeed, we need to get her all decked out. I'm sure Dee will help her with that."

Rome sighed, knowing that he had already given over to the idea of doing this undercover together. It was actually a great idea. He was known at the club, so a woman who would intrigue him would also grab the attention of the killer. That is, if he was hanging out at the club. Or around it.

"Okay, just make sure it doesn't get any further than you and Evan."

"And May and Chris and Cynthia."

Rome rolled his eyes. "Okay, but not outside the family."

Micah's lips twitched. "Sure. Guess we should head out. Why not come by the office tomorrow? I'll tell Evan to take the day off, and we can make sure all the security is up to date."

Rome nodded, knowing now there was no backing out.

. . . . .

Maria looked at the few tourists that walked down the streets of Honolulu and sighed with relief. "I guess this means you agree."

Rome said nothing as he turned onto Kalakaua Avenue and headed back to the hotel. There was no music, no noise inside the car. He'd barely said a word since Micah and Dee had left them alone. They'd talked over the case, but he hadn't talked unless it had to do with work.

Grinding her teeth together, she tried to keep her temper in check. She hated the silent treatment. It was something her father had used on her the few times she had rebelled against his plans for her. Days would go by without a word. It was enough to make a girl go crazy.

She shook those horrible memories away.

"Listen, I understand you might wonder if I am up to the task"

"I know you can do it."

Those few words spoken very softly told her that he really did believe it. She tried to fight the sharp sense happiness that his belief in her gave her, but it was hard. She worked with men who would never acknowledge her intelligence even if their life depended on it.

"Then why did you object?" she asked.

His hand tightened on the steering wheel. "I understand you know your job. But, you haven't been there. The torture this man gets off on, well, it isn't pleasant. I've seen the bodies. And if he finds out you're FBI, that will make you a prize."

"I've seen the photos, and believe it or not, I've been on several murder scenes. Hell, my father took me to my first one when I was sixteen."

"Your father let you go to a scene when you were a teenager?"

She fought the urge to defend her father. She knew Carino was trying to sidetrack her.

"Yeah." He opened his mouth, but she plowed ahead, trying to forestall any other questions on that subject. She needed his agreement on the plan or it wouldn't be as successful. Carino was the only backup she had on this case. That she'd ever had. She brushed that thought aside. "I have a feeling getting you interested in me will make me even more of a prize."

Rome slanted her a look that told her he was still pissed. "So that's another part of your plot."

Maria could tell it wasn't a question and just decided to let it go. He had agreed to do it. That was all she cared about. After a day or two, he would release the worry he had about it.

When they arrived at her hotel, she expected him to drop

her off at the front, but instead, he parked the car. After tossing his keys to the valet and grabbing the ticket, he took her by the elbow and headed to the Tapa Tower. Amazingly, they found themselves on the elevator alone.

"I don't care for your methods." She inwardly winced at her tone. She sounded like a prude.

He slanted her a look. "Yeah?"

"I understand you might not like it, but being a petulant child pouting over losing an argument doesn't make you look good. I won't take the silent treatment."

Before she knew what he was about, he grabbed her wrist, slipped in front of her, and then released her arm to cage her into the corner of the elevator.

"If you're going to play the submissive, you're going to have to be a little better at taking orders."

She couldn't speak. Her heart was beating so hard, she'd bet he could hear it. She raised her gaze from his chest to his face, and eventually made eye contact. Good God. Her whole body went on alert at the heat she saw flaming in the depths of his hazel eyes. She wasn't afraid of him, but the arousal that now slid through her body scared the bejesus out of her.

"You don't tell me what to do at the club. That'll tell people right off the bat you aren't serious about it. And if you want to play sub to my Dom, you better get used to doing exactly what I tell you."

He leaned forward, nuzzling her neck. His breath feathered out over her flesh, and she couldn't stop the shiver that racked her body. This kind of behavior shouldn't be turning her on. She didn't like 'take charge' kind of guys, and she definitely didn't like public displays. Apparently her body disagreed. Her nipples hardened and her breath tangled in her throat. She thought she felt his mouth on her skin, but the door dinged open, and he pulled back. It took her a second to yank herself out of the sea of lust he'd tossed her in. He stood by the door, keeping it open as if nothing strange had happened.

She drew in a deep breath, gathered up her senses and some of her pride, and stepped into the hallway. He walked behind her, a silent companion, but now her nerves were frazzled. What was it about this man? It wasn't that she felt she had to prove herself to him.

She stopped at her door and glanced back over her shoulder at him. "You didn't have to do that. I understand what's expected of me."

"Really?"

She fought back the irritation. "I've researched it. I would never suggest this if I didn't know what I had to do."

He nodded but still looked skeptical.

"I can play the role. You didn't have to pull that stunt."

He studied her for a moment, no expression on his face. Then, he placed his hand on the wall next to her head and leaned closer, as he did in the elevator. Gawd, he smelled good. Earthy and sensual, and all wrapped up in a dominant package of a man. She shouldn't want to attract him, but everything in her being was telling her to do anything to get him in her bed.

"What stunt are you talking about?"

For a moment, all she could do was look at his mouth as he spoke. His lips were full, sensual, and utterly irresistible.

"Callahan."

She shook herself and tried to remember what they had been talking about. Great, now she had to embarrass herself with an explanation. She didn't want to do this. She understood she wasn't attractive to men like Rome. That she could live with. Having to admit it to him out loud was more than a little awkward. Talk about humiliating.

"I understand that a woman like me would never attract you—"

"What do you mean by that?"

She glanced up and realized he looked genuinely surprised.

"Nothing. Just understand I can play a role, and I won't

get all sappy on you. I want this guy as much as you do."

Again he was silent. She hated that, hated the way he looked at her. It was as if he was completely perplexed by her. "Play a role?"

She rolled her eyes and pulled her keycard out, not able to look at him anymore. She was damned tired and ready to collapse. Add this embarrassment to the mix, and she just wanted to crawl under the covers and forget most of the day.

"When we're out of the public eye, I understand. You don't have to play the role of my lover behind the scenes. It'll be easier if we have parameters."

"Callahan." His voice was quiet nevertheless commanding.

"What?"

"Look at me." The order was soft but definitely not to be ignored. She couldn't if she'd wanted to. His deep, resonate voice wrapped around her senses and forced her to do his bidding.

When she finally made eye contact, her whole body went hot again. The intense look had her trying to swallow, but she found her mouth dry. He slipped his free hand up to cup her jaw. Without saying a word, he bent his head down and brushed his mouth against hers. She could feel the heat of him through their layers of clothing.

He leaned even closer, and she could feel his erection. There was no mistaking that. Just feeling the hot, long length of him had every hormone in her body jumping to attention, ready to serve. When he pulled back, it took a few moments for her to open her eyes again.

The fire in his eyes was still there. His cheeks were flushed, and she could tell there was a little more than just playacting involved.

"Just so you know. Guys like me can be attracted to women like you."

She nodded.

He kept his eyes opened this time as he gently brushed

his mouth over hers. Just that little touch had her circuits going crazy.

"Go in your room so I can leave."

She did as he ordered, without thinking about it until the door was shut and she was listening to his footsteps recede in the hallway. Dammit. What the hell was wrong with her? Her head was still spinning and her body humming. Closing her eyes, she tried to calm her out-of-control libido. The man was going to be a problem. She didn't get involved, it was a rule she'd had. Sure, there were a few one-nighters here and there, but they mostly didn't last, even if she wanted them to. Yearned for them more than she was willing to admit, even to herself.

She brushed that thought aside. She had learned the hard way that relationships and her just did not mix. Sitting down on her bed, she pulled off her shoes and started to unbutton her shirt. Her room phone rang.

She picked it up. "Hello."

"Having fun with locals?" Masters said, amusement in his voice.

Shit. "How long have you been a Peeping Tom, and does Gloria know about this?"

He chuckled. "I was wondering if you wanted to go over a few things since I'm heading out tomorrow."

She sighed, glanced at the bed. "Sure. Let me get something more comfortable on, and I'll be over."

"I've been wanting to hear that for years." He made kissy noises before he hung up. She was smiling when she put the phone back in the cradle. She'd realized that she'd misjudged Masters. He was an ass, and well, he didn't like many people. But he was the easiest partner she'd worked with at the bureau. Of course, he wasn't looking to make a name for himself. He was nearing twenty years in and ready to retire out of the FBI and do something else. He went through the motions and did what he had to do to make people think he was in for the long haul. And he respected her, although he did give her a hard time. Sort of like a big brother.

As she hurriedly undressed and threw on her workout clothes, she thought about Rome and what to do about him. She would just have to talk to him. Sure, they were playing lovers, but there was no need to do anything more. She would just tell him this was not going happen.

Because, if she thought about it, there was a good chance she'd definitely jump Rome's bones. And if she did that, she would definitely end up with a broken heart.

Chapter Four

The ticking of the clock was the only sound in Rough 'n Ready's office after Rome explained everything. Even though the room was cool, Rome barely registered it. He was boiling hot. On one hand, he wanted the partners to accept Callahan's idea. There was a good chance that the crazy ass plan might work. But it was that other hand that bothered him. Callahan was a competent agent. He'd checked her out that morning. He hoped that at least Evan would disagree, but Rome had known that was a long shot. Both men had been worried about the killings from the very first one and had been fully cooperative with the investigation. Their wives were well-known submissives at the club, so it was more than just protecting their name.

After a few more moments of silence, Evan leaned forward.

"You want to use the club for a sting?" he asked.

Rome knew that both partners would want all the information they could get on the operation. They might not have college degrees, but Rome hadn't met many men as business savvy as Evan Chambers and Micah Ross. They both started out life on the wrong side of the tracks, but they knew how to build a business and how to thrive. They would also be an asset to the investigation, had been from the start.

Rome nodded. "That's the plan. It wasn't my idea, but

there's a good chance it could work. No one but the captain and I know she's here to work. Her partner is going back to DC today."

"You're doing this outside the FBI, though. They think she's here to observe and offer guidance, correct?" Micah asked.

Rome rolled his shoulders. "Yes."

Micah looked at Evan. "He doesn't like it, but he doesn't have a choice."

"Does he think the woman can't do it?" Evan asked.

Micah shrugged. "Not sure. I do know he's attracted to her."

"Really?" Evan's eyes widened. "He has been in kind of a dry spell."

Rome's irritation soared. "Hey, jackasses, I'm right here."

They glanced at him then at each other and laughed.

He sighed, knowing they had done it on purpose to get under his skin. Ross and Chambers had grown up on the streets of Atlanta together, and their longstanding partnership allowed them to read each other well. In other words, they tended to be good at fucking with people. Especially him.

He pushed the thoughts aside and tried to concentrate on the business at hand. "I think she wants to start tonight."

"I know she does," Micah said. "She called Dee this morning about what she would need to fit in. She's shopping with May and Dee right now."

Evan raised his eyebrows. "Oh, that's who they were shopping with this morning. They said something about how sad it was that they couldn't make a trip to Maui Kink."

Rome felt his temper soaring. He kept it in check—barely. "There's no reason for that. What the hell are those two doing with her?"

Micah smiled, and Evan studied him. Rome ground his teeth together, knowing that both men were too perceptive to not pick up on the territorial note in his voice. Hell, if he could hear it, he knew they could.

"What I mean is that minimal expense needs to go into that. Knowing Callahan, she's footing the bill for the clothing."

"She's going to stay at the Hilton?" Micah asked, ignoring his lie.

"No. She said something about having a rental or something from the FBI."

And now that he said it, he realized he never asked her where she was going to be. It was a safe bet she would be out of the hotel today and in the house, and he had no freaking idea where that was. She had rattled him, and he didn't like it one bit.

Evan tsked. "He's not acting normal. He's usually on top of everything."

Micah nodded. "He was off last night, too. She really has thrown him for a loop."

"Who would have thought some fed would come in here and mess with the ever-organized Romeo Carino?"

Rome gave Evan the finger.

"Okay, so we'll put her name on the list. Is she using her real name?" Micah asked.

Shit. "We didn't go into that last night."

"What did you do last night?"

He could feel heat flare in his cheeks. Dammit, he was blushing again. He hadn't done this much blushing since puberty hit him. No one at Rough 'n Ready would believe it. Hell, no one at work would believe it.

"I took her back to her hotel room."

The partners shared a glance then looked back at him.

Aggravation inched down his spine. "What?"

"And what else happened?" Evan asked.

"Nothing. And if there had been anything, I wouldn't tell you. I would think you would appreciate my discretion."

Evan shook his head as his lips twitched.

"Let's get back to the problem at hand. You're worried

she might not be able to handle it?" Micah asked.

At first, he thought so. Now that he knew she'd researched the situation, he wasn't so sure. The way she'd handled herself the night before told him she was at least trained to handle situations like that. He shrugged. "According to her, she has done a lot of research."

"What kind of research?" Evan asked as he wiggled his eyebrows. "Was it hands on research?"

A wave of heat rolled through Rome at the thought. She said she had done research, read books, but truthfully, knowing her, she'd been to clubs. The idea that she might have done something with a Dom had his temper flaring. He didn't want another man to touch her. Just the thought had his anger heating to a dangerous level. And that thought had him worried.

"Ah, so you don't know. Knowing the woman, she did. She seems pretty thorough. And she has something to prove," Micah said.

"What are you talking about?" Evan asked.

"Father is that big serial killer hunter you always wanted to meet."

"You wanted to meet Big John Callahan?" Rome asked.

Evan shrugged, looking a little embarrassed. "I just thought it would be cool."

"He was."

"You met him?" Evan asked.

"Went to a few of his lectures when I was stationed in DC."

Evan looked like he wanted to ask more questions, but Micah steered them back to the topic at hand again. "Y'all are going to start tonight? Got a plan?"

Rome wanted to curse. He hated that a lot of this could have been discussed the night before. Of course, he hadn't been able to think of anything else beyond touching Maria. "No, but I'm sure she has one. She has no problem telling me what to do."

"At least you get to reverse that tonight."

Micah's comment sent a rush of heat through his blood, had his body reacting before he could stop it. Rome knew it was all about undercover. But there was the problem of their attraction. She might try to pretend she wasn't attracted to him, but he had felt the way she had trembled when he touched her the night before. Hell, he could still taste her on his lips. He'd never really had this kind of response to a woman before. Not since high school. It was as if he couldn't control himself.

The thought that she would be in the club, dressed to attract, had him sweating. He wasn't sure he would survive the night.

· · · · ·

Maria looked at herself in the mirror and blinked. The dress May had picked out clung to her curves and accentuated her hips. The push-up bra…well it did its job well. She blinked again. She didn't recognize herself. Her face looked the same, but her body…she felt almost naked.

"Come out, we want to see."

Maria frowned as she smoothed her hands over her hips. "I'm not so sure about this."

The curtain opened, and Dee stood there. Her eyes widened as her gaze took in the way the dress fit Maria. "Wow!"

Horrified, Maria gasped. "I could have been naked."

"If you were in here alone all this time naked, I would be wondering what you were doing," May said. The woman had a sassy sense of humor that appealed to Maria. She seemed to say the things that Maria thought but didn't have the nerve to say out loud.

"I say you'll grab the attention of more than one guy tonight. Especially Rome," May said. "He likes a full ass, doesn't he Dee."

"That really isn't that important," she said even as a tiny little thrill zinged through her. She shouldn't be that excited that Rome apparently went for her body type.

"Sure it is. You want to attract men, right? Which, with this tiny waist and that rear end of yours, especially in this dress, you will. As I said, Rome likes some booty," May said, giving hers a little wiggle.

Maria cleared her throat as her face burned. She was an adult, but she had spent little time around women. She was always mystified by the openness of their discussions, especially these two women.

Dee nodded. "Yeah, he does. I watch him watch women, and those are the ones he always goes for. He's going to be dying when he sees you in this."

Maria was shaking her head. She couldn't fall for the fantasy they were creating—no matter how much she wanted it to be true. And it was best to lay it out so these women understood the situation.

"Whether or not he finds me attractive isn't a concern for me." Not really. "That's not that important. We just have to pretend."

The women shared a look and then looked at her. "From what Dee said last night, there was no pretending on Rome's end."

Before she could respond to that, Dee said, "Turn around."

Maria did as ordered and then cursed herself again. She let the little woman order her around like she was some kind of dress up doll.

Without permission, May tugged at the bodice of the dress, pulling the neckline further down. "Oh, yeah, that's the perfect cut on the top. Your boobs look great with the push-up."

Embarrassment had her cheeks turning red again. The longer she knew them, the worse they seemed to get. It had only been a couple of hours. What would they be like after she had known them for a whole week? Did all women talk like this? She wasn't really sure. Her mother died when she was twelve, and she had very few female friends. Men didn't talk this way about clothes. And they definitely couldn't make as many comments about her boobs as May Chambers had or the agent would be slapped with a sexual harassment filing.

Dee sighed. "May, you're being a little…well, May."

May looked at Dee then back at Maria. "Oh, sorry. I didn't mean to overwhelm you."

Dee laughed. "May does that a lot. But I have to say, that dress is exactly what you need."

Maria frowned and glanced at the image of her backside. "Are you sure? I've never been someone who wore such loud colors."

"Red isn't loud, it's colorful," May said as if what she said made sense.

"Don't most people wear black?" she asked. "The two clubs I went to in DC seemed to be filled with black leather."

Dee nodded. "This will help you stand out a little more, which is exactly what you're wanting to do. Besides, that color makes your skin look like porcelain."

"If you two say so, I'll go with it."

"Now, we need to do something with all that hair of yours," Dee said.

She was eyeing Maria's bun as if it was offensive. Maria really didn't want to do anything with her hair, so she decided to change the subject.

"Don't I need jewelry?"

"No, with a dress like that, you don't want them to look at anything but you," May said. "I think we need a *mallassada* break. And we can talk about hair."

The thought of girl talk usually sent her running in the other direction, but this, she knew, would help her. She needed to attract the killer, and she needed their help. She'd have to trust them and Rome to get this bastard. And, if it meant decking herself out like a sex toy waiting to be played with, she would do it.

. . . . .

Rome got to the club about ten that night. After his embarrassment with the guys, he'd called Maria, and they had set up their sting. Not that he had much to say about the plans. He'd talked to Maria a few times that day, but he had yet to see her. He couldn't explain the churning in his gut. It wasn't the usual adrenaline rush he got from police work. There had been a time that he loved to do undercover. And there was a part of him that still did. But this was different. This involved a women who tangled him up like none other.

He noticed a few of the regulars, talked to a few people as he walked through the crowd. It had to look casual, as if he were here for a typical night at Rough 'n Ready. When he reached the bar, Dee was smiling at him. "Good evening, Detective Carino."

He couldn't help but return the smile. Dee Ross was a tough woman, but she had a softer side to her that always appealed to him. Not sexually, but more like a little sister. She actually reminded him of his younger sister, so that was probably why. All hardass, but that soft core made her a heck of a woman.

"Busy for a Tuesday," he commented.

She nodded as she fixed his drink. Non-alcoholic, not because of work, but because of the policy of the club. Micah had always had control on the drinking, but after a few problems, he and Evan had decided to cut out any alcohol for anyone who was going into the rooms in the back. Playing at Rough 'n Ready was done alcohol free. Without a black wristband, you couldn't get into the rooms. Rome's wristband felt like a lead weight as he glanced around the area looking for Callahan.

"Yeah. I'm a little surprised. I figured we would lose a few people to the club we opened on the North Shore, but it seemed to increase our membership here."

He nodded, really not listening. *Where was Callahan?* She said she would be there by ten. Callahan could be counted on, he knew that. He could tell from the way she methodically planned this that she was ready to go after the guy. He looked over the crowd, seeing a few more familiar faces...and a lot of new ones. Dee was right. There were a lot of new people which was a problem for the investigation. He noted a cluster of people just on the other side of the dance floor. There seemed to be a few people watching, a few people conversing, and in the center, there was a woman. He didn't know how he knew, but there was a woman. Someone shifted, and he saw her then. Her back was to him. Most of the back of the dress was gone, not there. It showed off all her perfect ivory skin. Dark curls dripped over her shoulders. He dropped his gaze down to her ass. Lord have mercy. Full, curved...he could just imagine the way it would feel beneath his fingers.

He took a step in the woman's direction and stopped. What the hell was he doing? He was here to hunt a serial killer with Callahan. Who he needed to find. Just as he turned away, the woman laughed and turned toward one of the men fawning on her. He couldn't see her face fully, but he recognized the curve of her jaw and those sculpted cheekbones. A jolt of recognition went through him.

And on the crest of the wave of that came a possessiveness that he could barely contain. He felt a rumble in his chest, and he realized he actually growled.

He stepped in her direction but stopped when a massive hand clamped down on his shoulder. Rome turned to tell whoever it was to piss off when he found himself staring at a very amused Micah.

"Might want to play a little harder to get there, Carino."

"Fuck off."

Micah just laughed and patted him on the back. "Happy hunting...and be careful."

He nodded, knowing that Micah was just as worried about the operation as Rome was. The partners had agreed, but both of them were worried about Callahan's safety.

Rome started off in her direction, again determined to make sure she understood that her behavior wasn't even close to acceptable. And if she didn't understand that, he would take her some place private and make sure she did.

Chapter Five

Maria could feel something invisible brush the back of her neck. It tingled as if someone had slid their fingers over the fine hairs, but she knew no one was touching her. Which meant people were watching her. Someone in particular. Fighting the shiver it caused, she took a sip of her virgin Lava Flow and looked around the room as casually as possible. She didn't recognize anyone other than the few people she'd talked to. Something had her looking over her shoulder.

Rome.

He was bearing down on her little group of men. She couldn't fight the heat that flared low in the belly, or the way her heart turned over at the sight of him striding through the club. In a place where there were Doms aplenty, people stepped out of his way. He didn't push or shove. He just walked, and something in their subconscious told them to move. The closer he got, the faster her pulse raced.

She turned her attention back to the group surrounding her. Getting her bearings straight to do the investigation was important. She'd worked undercover, so she could hide her discomfort with the gathering, but it was hard. Never before had she attracted this much attention. May had introduced her to two men and then left her alone as soon as the other men descended.

"So, Maria, you're not from the islands?" a man asked.

She focused on him, or tried to. He was tall and lean, with a hint of public school British accent. From her training, she picked up on the fact that it was fake, as were his capped teeth and sun-tipped hair. He probably had paid a fortune to a stylist to get it to look that natural. Dammit, she couldn't remember his name. She needed to because it was part of her job. But knowing Rome was on his way to her had her brain scrambled.

"No. I'm just here for a week or two visiting. I heard about Rough 'n Ready from a friend in DC."

Her father had taught her how to lie. *Make sure you wrapped it in truth so you don't screw up and reveal something more about yourself.*

"I thought I hadn't seen you before," he said as he inched closer, not noticeably, but enough to make her uncomfortable. He was good looking, but there was something very calculating in his brown eyes. Something that told her that he had more interest in her than was healthy. Dammit, she needed to remember his name.

"Of course you haven't, Ashton," Rome rumbled from behind her. "You only show interest in the new subs."

There was an acute silence and then Ashton snarled before he could hide it from her. In the next instant, he smoothed his features. *Hiding a temper, are you?*

"Excuse the ruffian behind you, my dear. He's one of our public servants."

The way he said it told her he thought less of people who worked to keep him safe. Jackass. She wanted so badly to knee the idiot in his groin, but she kept herself from performing the task. Somehow Rome insinuated himself into the space beside her.

"I was wondering if the lady would like to dance?"

She turned toward him, and the impact was even more powerful than before. A blast of heat surged through her entire body. Her lips started to tingle as she remembered the way he had kissed her the night before.

"Sure," she said without looking away from him. She shoved her glass at Ashton as Rome took her hand and led her out onto the dance floor.

Even though it was cool in the club, she felt her body start to warm being so close to him. Rome let off so much heat. He stopped and pulled her closer as a slow song started. Damn, she wasn't prepared for the impact of having his entire body against hers.

He leaned down, his lips against her temple. "Got yourself quite a little harem there."

She tried to adjust to the fact that she was this close to him again. The rumble of his chest as he spoke had her shivering. Maria knew he could probably feel her hardened nipples.

It took a second for the irritation in his voice to reach her. She pulled her head from his shoulder and looked up at him. He wasn't looking at her. He was looking out over the crowd.

"That was the plan, wasn't it?"

He grumbled something, and his chest rumbled against her again. With the music so loud, she couldn't make out what he said.

Before she could ask, he said, "Ashton isn't the killer."

She blinked at the change in topic. "Shouldn't we wait to talk about that? Maybe you should ask me my name? Or act like you want to be dancing with me? You've barely looked at me."

He glanced down at her then back out at the crowd again. The hand on the small of her back pressed her closer. She could feel his erection then. Every thought in her brain seemed to fizzle away.

"If I look down at you, I might not be able to control myself."

She scoffed at that. "Oh, yeah, Carino, why don't you pull my other leg? I know your type, and you are all about control. Hell, you practice BDSM, so don't think I don't know a Dom like you is into control."

His jaw flexed slightly. If she hadn't been watching him, she would have missed it. It was definitely his one big tell.

"I can't."

For a second, she wasn't sure she heard him correctly. "What?"

He sighed, aggravation filling the sound. Why was that sexy to her? She knew she was pushing him, pressing buttons. That thought made her wiggle her hips ever so slightly, causing her stomach to move against his erection more. He growled, and she smiled.

He slipped his hands down to her hips and tried to hold her still. "Stop that."

"Whatcha gonna do?"

She was surprised by the teasing sound in her voice, but she couldn't help it. He brought it out in her. He looked down at her, his hazel eyes dark with lust.

"Stop. Or maybe I can take you into one of the rooms and show you just how it feels to publically submit."

Heat rushed through her at the image he brought up. She shifted slightly and felt the dampness of her panties. Lord, she was soaking wet. Need throbbed in her veins. The desire that threaded his voice had her body yearning to do just what he suggested. Maria knew she would never be able to do it, and that would go above and beyond the call of duty, but dammit, it sounded utterly delicious. She licked her lower lip.

"Jesus," he muttered. He slipped his hand up her back to her head then he pressed it closer, forcing her to settle it against his shoulder. "We can't leave right now. So stop looking at me like that."

"Like what?"

He sighed. This time his whole chest moved. She had the feeling he was trying to control his temper.

"You know exactly what I'm talking about."

She didn't, but she figured that most women would. Okay, so she knew she was pushing some buttons, but just how did she look at him? Before she could figure out the answer to her question, the song ended.

Instead of leading her back to where she was, he led her over to the bar. Micah was there and smiled at her as they approached. In the exotic environment of his club, the Native American Dom looked even more beautiful.

"Evening, Maria," Micah said, then he winked. "I do believe that is the first time I've seen Romeo out on the floor."

"Fuck off, Micah," Rome said as he sat down on a stool and pulled her against him. He did it with such force that she stumbled back. But soon her back was pressed against his chest. She glanced around and found everyone avidly watching them. She leaned back.

"You're making a spectacle out of me."

"You don't like it? You seemed to like it earlier." He was silent for a second or two. "And if you didn't like people looking at you, you might have spent a little more money to get more material added to that excuse of a dress you're wearing."

She didn't have a clue what he was talking about, but from his surly tone, she wasn't about to find out. Besides, she could barely think straight. His hand kept rubbing against her stomach. With each brush, he moved closer to her breasts. She wasn't used to public displays, and she hoped people didn't see her blush. It wouldn't bode well for their investigation.

"You're coming on a little strong."

"There's nothing little about it," he said, amusement filling his voice. "Admit it. You like the idea that people are watching me touch you."

She couldn't admit it to him. Wouldn't. But she did. Lord how she did. Her body was already hot from being close to him, from dancing. Now, though, the idea that people were somehow interested in them made her hot. It wasn't a normal feeling for her. She usually had short, casual affairs, and whether it was another agent or not, it never took place in public. She liked to have some discretion in her relationships. She definitely didn't allow a man to touch her like this in public.

But she really liked it. A lot.

"I bet you would like to publically submit, wouldn't you? Being stripped naked in front of all these people…tied up…spanked."

His voice deepened with each word. She closed her eyes and shivered. He said something low and explicit under his breath. She wasn't sure just what it was, but the image he painted made her need. She needed to be touched, to be held, to do all those things he'd offered. The beat of the music pounded through her blood, intertwined with the lust he inspired.

Abruptly he stood, and without a word to her, he said to Micah, "See ya later."

And with that, he pulled her out of the club and into the night. At the moment, the only thing on her mind was if they would actually make it to her rented house before he made good on his threats.

· · · · ·

Lust wound through his blood and was definitely scrambling his brain. He had never been this mixed up about a woman. Not even his grade school crush on Marjorie Wickers had left him this crazed. He got to the car and realized she was frowning at him. On top of it, he knew it was best they went to the house that the FBI had rented for her. It was probably in the Honolulu area and not on the other side of the island, like his.

"What?" he asked.

"What was that all about?"

She was going to be a pain in the ass. Women like her

always were. They wanted schedules, explanations, just wanted too much. But that didn't matter at the moment. His brain was barely functioning, and he could hardly keep from taking her in the parking lot. He stepped closer, crowding her up against his car.

"Listen, Callahan. I know part of what you were doing in there was an act. But you went over the line, way over the line. You have five seconds to tell me no. After that, you're mine for the night."

She swallowed, and he could see the flush of embarrassment—or was it arousal—brighten her eyes. Her tongue slipped out over her plump lower lip. He growled and leaned in for a taste. Just like the night before, he was drawn in by the kiss. A simple brush of the mouth turned into something completely carnal when she opened her mouth to him. He stole inside. By the time he drew back, they were both breathing heavily.

He rested his forehead against hers. She drew in a deep, shuttering breath. It caused her breasts to press against his chest. Jesus. He knew from the way the fabric clung to her ass, she wasn't wearing panties. It wouldn't take much to push the fabric over those full hips of hers and take her in the parking lot. From the dazed look in her blue eyes, he might just be able to do it.

He curled his fingers against the roof of his car.

"Yes or no."

She studied him for a second, although if felt like an eternity. She drew in another shuddering breath.

"Yes."

Chapter Six

He gave her another hard, quick kiss then unlocked the car. By the time he was driving down Ala Wai Boulevard, he realized he didn't know where her rental was.

"Where's your house?"

She rattled off the address, and he knew it was faster to get there than his house over in Laie. Even on a Monday night, it would take a good forty minutes. He didn't think he would last that long. Hell, he was lucky he was going to be able to make it over to Kahala.

It took less than fifteen minutes to drive to her rental. He turned off the car and tried to calm the libido he seemed to not be able to control around her. After his issues in Seattle, he had discovered BDSM. Control had become very important to him, in and out of the bedroom. Now, though, all those lessons seemed to fail him. He felt...wired. It was as if he'd had forty ounces of coffee pumped into his blood.

"Rome?"

He looked at her and realized he'd been sitting there for a few moments without saying anything. She'd left her porch light on, and the glow from it allowed him to see the scandalous dress she was wearing. The moment he saw her wearing it, he had been itching to take if off. And for the first time in years, he had felt the bone deep need to possess. Not just dominate. This went beyond that. He had never wanted to possess someone so forcefully. It scared the living hell out of him, but he seemed helpless to ignore the thrum of lust churning his gut.

She sighed, the sound kind of sad and lonely. "It's okay. Why don't we meet up in the morning?"

He frowned. His brain wasn't really working well, so he couldn't follow her line of thought. Hell, he couldn't remember his name at the moment. "What?"

She frowned, and a look of irritation moved over her face. Oh, way to blow her away with your conversation skills, Carino. No man in his right mind would blame him, though. He had no brain cells left. They'd been evaporated since seeing her in the club. What was she expecting, wearing a dress like that?

"I said it's okay. I'll see you in the morning."

She was heading to her front door before he could react. He got out of his car and followed her. She looked around at him with wide eyes. She had her door opened, and he gently eased her into her house then shut the door and locked it.

"You said yes."

She studied him for a second again. He hated that. He knew she was weighing and measuring everything. Considering who her father was, there was a good chance she'd been raised to do just that. Rome did it himself. Still, it didn't seem right. Maria seemed to analyze everything he might be feeling…what he said. That pissed him off.

"I did, but I thought you changed your mind."

He cocked his head to the side. "Why would I?"

She shrugged. There was something different in her manner. Then it struck him. For the first time since meeting her, she looked vulnerable. She wasn't so sure of herself in this situation. In work, she was confident. Almost overly so, if you asked him. It was one of the reasons she had come up with the plan. She never doubted herself. But in this she did. It eased his temper a bit and gave him a warm feeling in his chest.

"You think everything was an act?" She shrugged again and wouldn't meet his gaze. "Look at me."

She didn't do it fast enough.

"Now." His voice lashed out, but he couldn't help it. This woman had twisted him up, and worse, she had no idea what she had done to him. She actually thought he was acting. When her blue gaze finally met his, he knew she hadn't been playing him.

"First, when I tell you to do something, you do it."

From the way her mouth turned down, she didn't like that order one bit.

"And seriously, do you think I could act good enough that I could pretend to be so aroused, I'm walking around with an erection constantly?"

She dropped her gaze from his, and he felt it as if it had been a lick. His cock pulsed and then twitched. He counted backwards from ten—three times.

"Maria."

She looked at him.

"You said yes."

She nodded.

"Do you understand what that means, what it entails?"

"I read up on BDSM for the case, Rome." It was the first time she'd said his name. He was almost giddy from the sound of her voice rolling over the letters. He was in serious trouble.

"Reading about it is something different than experiencing it."

"Do you think I can't handle it?"

She didn't look so vulnerable right now. In fact, she looked ready to conquer worlds. He found he liked both of the Marias. The one who made him want to soothe her worries and the warrior queen in front of him.

"Oh, I think you can handle it. And I know you would like it, Maria. I saw your reaction to my order earlier. Pick a safe word."

She licked her lips again, that tongue darting out over her plump lips. Inwardly he groaned, but he didn't have as much control over it as he thought. There was a rumble in his chest. Just the thought of sliding his cock between her lips had him barely able to think straight.

"Flower."

Without another word, he stepped forward, grabbed her hand and walked her down the hall to the bedroom.

"Which one?" he asked, hoping she knew what he meant.

"Last one on the left."

He got her into the room without too many issues. He ignored the urge to take her there, strip her naked, plunge into her body. At least he tried to. Later, he knew he would marvel at the fact that he could walk standing up and not crawl on the floor begging her for sex. But right now, in this, he could at least attempt to be the Dom he was.

The room was nondescript, except for the bed. Damn, the thing was huge. It had to be a California king. There would be lots of room to move and play. He let go of her hand and sat on the bed. She stood in front of him. The dim light from the hallway was not enough.

"Turn on the light."

She did as ordered.

"Come back over here, Maria."

As she walked toward him, he was struck by her looks again. She'd been a somewhat attractive woman before, but that dress had shown what she had been hiding. Full, tight, and definitely womanly. But it went beyond that. He had noted the ivory skin, the way her blue eyes seemed to take up her whole face, and he definitely noted the bee-stung lips. But the hair, that had him itching to run his fingers through it.

"Still sure?"

She nodded.

"Do not speak unless spoken to. The only time you do is if you need to say your safe word. Nothing but answers to my questions. Do you understand?"

"Yes."

Another zing of anticipation swept through him. It was her first time, so he knew he couldn't ask for a complete submission. He didn't have any toys with him, and he didn't have his preferred restraints. He settled back on the bed and tried to calm his racing heart. He had never been this excited by a sub's agreement. She didn't like it, not one bit, but she definitely was going to do it.

"Strip down to your panties and bra."

She hesitated. He could understand. It was a big thing to ask of someone new to the game, but he felt the need to gain complete control over her. Something deep-seated in him told him he needed to be the one in charge from the beginning. She wouldn't respect him otherwise.

Then she reached up and untied the top of her dress. He expected her to take her time, but she let it fall into a pool at her feet. For a second, he didn't say anything. He was sure he didn't show any kind of reaction to her, or he hoped. The wild beast inside him wanted to howl because, damn, the woman was beyond gorgeous.

She was wearing a push-up bra, red, along with a pair of panties, although they might not be called panties. He was sure there was some kind of requirement in amount of material. This was definitely lacking in that department. He could tell it was a thong, but he didn't have her turn around. His palms were sweating, his body screaming. He did his best again not to show any reaction. He was in control...he hoped. She had not one mark on her skin, except for a tiny scar on her shoulder. He could tell from the way it looked it was a bullet wound, but he decided to wait until later to ask her about that.

"Turn around."

She did so without hesitation, and his dominant side rejoiced. She was definitely an Alpha female every day of the week at work—she had displayed that when he first met her. But from the small amount he had seen of her in the bedroom, Rome knew she had the makings of an excellent sub.

"Stop," he ordered when she had turned completely away from him.

She did as ordered, giving him a full view of her ass. His tongue stuck to the top of his mouth, and his mind went completely blank. He had always liked a full ass on a woman. Breasts, he liked them just a handful, but an ass, he liked that full and heart-shaped. And damned if Maria didn't fit that requirement. The thong was perfect for viewing, of course. Dammit. He curled his fingers into the palms of his hands, trying to quell the urge to spank her red right now. He could just imagine how pink her flesh would get. Since she wasn't looking, he licked his lips. All the woman was doing was standing there in her bra and panties, and she had him slavering like a beast.

He couldn't completely resist touching her. From experience, he knew how soft her skin was, but he needed to touch, taste. It was too much to ask him to wait any longer. He walked up behind her and stood so close he knew she could feel his chest against her back. He slipped his hand down her spine, easily unhooking her bra, then continuing to her ass. Damn, it was like touching the softest silk.

She shivered in reaction, and he felt it to the core of his soul. It wasn't anything that big, nothing that would mean much to other people. But the small response struck him hard and fast.

"You've been to clubs, yes?"

She nodded as he cupped one of her ass cheeks. God, he almost lost it then and there. He wanted so much from her, too much. He didn't understand his response. The attraction, yes. That was easy to appreciate. It was the almost overwhelming need he felt churning in his gut that had him worried. This went beyond simple attraction. It had him itching from the inside out. There was a part of him that worried this was all an experiment with her. Many people went undercover and had to live the life. They couldn't perform their job any other way. Another person in Maria's position might go along with submission to get Rome to feel closer, to bond. But something told him that she was doing it for herself.

He pulled himself out of his musings and back to the woman causing all the problems.

"Did you participate?"

He asked the question, not wanting to hear the answer.

"No."

The simple answer made him smile. It had come out just like a perfect little sub should answer her Dom. A possessiveness he didn't expect slapped him in the face, and he had to fight the urge to claim her. It wacked him upside the head like the club he should be carrying. It was primitive, Neanderthal almost. But he could stem the rising tide to make her understand just who she belonged to. Shit, this wasn't a long-term relationship. He knew it was more than just the job, knew that for both of them it was. Rome just needed to remind himself that this wasn't for keeps. He had met her less than forty-eight hours ago. She would be gone as soon as her job was done.

He bit down on the need to deny her the right to leave him. Fuck, he had to get his mind back into her submission and off any kind of relationship. He didn't have any claim to her for the long term. But for the short term, he could make her his in a way she would never forget.

He trailed his fingers over her generous flesh. He never would have guessed her ass was so shapely before seeing it in that dress. Without hesitation, he pulled his hand back and gave her a smack. Her gasp filled the silence in the air. Rome heard the arousal, the surprise, and he couldn't help doing it again. From his training, he knew just what it did to her, how the vibrations feathered out over the skin and throughout her body. He gave her another slap and smiled. He'd been right. Her skin pinkened so pretty.

67

Rome stepped in front of her. He crowded her, but she stood her ground. He could fight the little smile that brought about. He could smell the faint scent of her soap and her desire. It was a heady mixture. She was staring at the floor. Slipping a finger beneath her chin, he raised it to force her to look at him. Her lips were full with that bee-stung look that actresses paid a fortune to achieve. He dipped his head and brushed his mouth over hers. He'd been thinking of doing this—plus a whole lot more—since he'd touched her the night before.

One kiss was not enough. Rome had known it wouldn't be. He slid his tongue along the seam of her lips, and she opened them willingly. She didn't even hesitate for a second. Once he stole inside, she moaned. Tiny vibrations tingled over his tongue then filtered throughout his body. By the time he pulled back, the simple kiss had left them both breathing heavily.

Maria returned her gaze to the floor. "Look at me." He waited until she had before continuing. "You don't have to show me deference like that. It's not my thing."

He dropped his hand and was happy to see that she held his gaze. He slipped her bra off then placed it on the bureau behind him. He turned back around and sighed. She was just perfect. Small, delicate breasts were tipped with hardened pink nipples. She wasn't big, but that was his preference.

He cupped one, brushing his thumb over the tip. She sucked in a deep breath but seemed reluctant to do so.

"Show your pleasure. I like that." He bent down and licked her nipple. "But," he warned, looking up at her, "do not come unless I give you permission. You will do everything I tell you. You will let me know the pleasure I give you, but you do not allow yourself that pleasure. It's mine to own and mine to offer."

He had meant to keep his voice modulated, but by the end of the orders, he was grinding out each word. He couldn't seem to keep himself from letting her know he would own her body and soul.

He took the tip of her nipple in his mouth, grazing his teeth over it, suckling one and then the other. They hardened further. God, she was so fucking responsive. He never would have believed a woman who seemed so in control of her life, so, well, Alpha in her work, would be such a good little sub. But he knew she would be…at least for him. Damn if that didn't get him harder. He pinched her nipples, enjoying the way she moaned. When he took another tip back into his mouth, sucking hard, her knees buckled a bit.

He chuckled as he moved away from her. "Why don't you lay on the bed, Maria? Face up. Oh, and take off those panties and spread your legs."

She hesitated for just a second but did as he ordered without another admonition. He knew this was hard, harder than most people would understand. This first time, a sub had no idea what they would gain. For a sub, he knew after their first time with a true Dom, they would know what was coming, how much more their pleasure would be when they gave their trust to someone else. Researching it didn't count. No matter how much you read about it or watched other people go through it, you never knew how it felt.

He pulled off his shirt, keeping his back to the bed. He thought if he looked at her now with outstretched legs, he might lose control. He could just imagine that little pink pussy wet with her desire. By the time he turned around, he was as naked as she was. Even with all that extra time to compose himself, he felt his control slipping when he saw her.

"Put your feet on the bed, bend your legs."

When she did, he had to fight back a groan. She was wet, beyond wet, and he hadn't really touched her. Her pussy lips were glistening with her arousal.

He set the condom he'd pulled from his wallet on the bedside table and then joined her on the bed, settling beside her hip. She was watching him, her gaze wide with interest and the deep blue of her eyes dark with her arousal. He trailed a finger down her stomach, enjoyed the way it jumped at the contact. When he rested his palm against her sex, he couldn't fight the groan. She was wet and warm, and he could just imagine how it would feel to slip his cock into her. He brushed his thumb against her clit and saw her legs tense up.

"I told you not to hide your pleasure." He pressed against her clit hard, and she moaned then. Long and low. "Better."

To reward her for doing as he said, he bent his head between her legs and gave her pussy one long lick. Just that one taste had him craving another, but he took his time. He rose from the bed and walked to the foot of it. He wanted more, wanted to play more, do more, but that wasn't for tonight. But there would be other nights. That he promised himself. She might not be his to keep forever, but he damned sure was going to indulge himself while she was.

He crawled between her legs and breathed in the scent of her. Damn. She was exotic, soft ivory skin, dark, dark hair. She was looking down at him, those gorgeous blue eyes framed by dark lashes, and for a moment, he couldn't think. His brain just shut off.

Then, in the next instant, the lust that had been twining through his veins exploded. He pulled back the beast that clawed at his gut and dipped his head for another taste of her sweet pussy. He slipped his tongue in again, enjoying the little gasp of excitement that escaped her lips. Running his tongue up to her clit, he slid his finger into her, enjoying the way her muscles clung to it. Her legs moved against his head, her moans growing louder and louder. He added a second finger as he took her clit between his teeth. She quivered, her body bowing, but he pulled back before she could come. Her aggravated groan made him smile. He looked up at her. She was a joy to behold. She might not have said a word, but her eyes were spitting blue fire.

"I didn't give you permission to come yet," he said, then

lightly tapped her pussy. She shuddered and bit her lip.

He kissed each of her thighs, licking the soft flesh, enjoying the taste of her. Slowly, he worked his way up her body, dipping his tongue into her belly button, then sliding up to her breasts. She was a delight of curves and fragrant skin. He lay on top of her, enjoying the way she fit perfectly beneath him. The heat of her sex warmed his cock, causing it to twitch. He wanted to take more time, demand a complete submission, but that wasn't in the cards tonight. Even an experienced sub would refuse that. It didn't keep him from wanting it from her, yearning for it on a level that left him feeling vulnerable. He pushed the thought aside as he rose to his hands and looked down at her. The breath he'd been drawing in clogged his throat as he felt everything in the world fade away but her. She was looking at him with a strange mixture of arousal and wariness. He gave her another kiss, slipping his tongue between her lips and allowing her to taste herself. She needed to know just how delectable she was to him. How good she tasted. He pulled back, ready to take her, but remembered he needed a condom. Rome pulled himself up and grabbed the condom he'd set on the table. He ripped it open and had it on in record time.

He moved back between her legs. When he looked down at her, he had to count backwards from ten again. How did he end up so lucky? The woman was exactly his type. All that dark hair spread out over the ivory sheets, her lips even more swollen from his kissing, and her eyes heavy with lust. Rome gave her a slow, easy kiss that had his heart thudding hard and his need for her out of control. He rose up to his knees, pulled her hips up and then entered her in one hard thrust.

Fucking hell. It was the only thing that came to mind. It wasn't exactly romantic, but it was what it was. Her muscles clung to him as he pulled himself back out and thrust back in.

"Wrap your legs around my waist," he ordered, and she immediately complied. His orgasm approached, but he wanted to give her hers first. "Maria. Come for me, beautiful."

She thrashed her head back and forth.

He reached down between them, teased her clit. "Come for me, do it now, Maria."

In that next instant, she convulsed, bowing up to meet his thrusts as she screamed his name. Her orgasm pulled him further into her warmth, dragging his orgasm from him. One last thrust and he lost it, allowing his orgasm to take over.

He collapsed on top of her. He felt her lips brush over his shoulder. Pulling back, he looked down at her. Her eyes were closed, and a small smile curved her lips.

"I believe that you and I were both wrong, Maria. You are a submissive."

She chuckled. "I guess we were wrong." She opened her eyes. The lazy satiated look made him smile. "And thank the good lord for that."

Chapter Seven

Maria stretched then snuggled down into the comfort of her bed. Lord, she was tired. Her muscles felt like she'd been through a fight of some sort. And, for once, she wasn't ready to get out of bed and get to work. She just wanted to lay around and be lazy.

"Do you always sleep this late?"

She slowly opened her eyes and found Rome lounging by the door. He was dressed in his pants, which were zipped but not buttoned. And, damn, he looked as sexy as he had the night before. Which she was sure she did not.

"Maria?"

"Huh?"

Damn, the man had a chest on him. He definitely worked out, although some of it was just in the genes. He had a spattering of hair across his pecs, and she liked that. Then, there was a thin line of dark hair all the way down to his belly button. She worked out with FBI agents who couldn't hold a candle to the abs on Rome. Hell, she could probably bounce a quarter off the smooth, defined surface.

"Maria, look at me."

"I am."

He sighed. "You keep looking at me like that and you won't ever make it out of this bedroom today."

Her gaze dropped to his crotch, and she felt heat fill her

face. It wasn't hard to see his arousal. She cleared her throat and raised her gaze to his. Instead of being mad, he had a self-depreciating smile curving his lips

"You're right," she said.

"You have nothing to eat here for breakfast."

She glanced up at him. "If you let me get ready, we can go out. I didn't have time to shop for food."

"Okay."

But he kept standing there. She was proud of her body, but good lord, it was the morning after. He wasn't supposed to just stand there and watch. He was supposed to leave her alone for a few minutes. Didn't the man understand that? Apparently not because he kept standing there waiting for her.

"You can go to the living room."

His lips curved. "I know. Like the scenery here better."

She huffed out a sigh. "Carino, I'm asking for some privacy."

"And I'm denying it. Besides, I don't like being called Carino. I like it when you call me Rome."

"Then quit acting like a jackass."

He chuckled and pushed away from the doorjamb. "Come on, Maria, there's no reason to be so shy. Not with that body."

She pulled the sheet up higher. "I just need time." To figure out what the hell happened last night, for one thing. Then she needed to formulate a plan to deal with it.

"Thinking is overrated." His voice was deepening, and she could tell that he was flirting with her. But she was never good at this. She was never good at any of it. She never knew what men expected the morning after. Not that there had been that many morning afters.

Before she could assimilate what she needed to do, he was beside the bed and tugging at the sheet. He pulled her gently from the bed and led her to the small bathroom. Before she could shut the door, he gave her a soft, easy kiss.

"Morning, Maria."

Just hearing her name on his lips sent heat coursing through her veins. What the hell was she doing with a man who could do this to her with a small kiss? She couldn't compete with that, couldn't even fathom being able to interest him longer than a night. But apparently he was.

"I—I need to get ready."

He nodded and stepped back, allowing her to close the door. She waited until she heard his footsteps fade away and then she let out a breath she didn't know she was holding. He had her head all screwed up with him. She couldn't think straight, and that wasn't good when she was on one of the most important jobs of her career. This assignment would solidify that she was an agent in her own right. If she fucked it up, she was, well, fucked. She would never be able to overcome the idea that she had her position because of her father and his friends.

She shook those worries away. There was one thing she was good at and that was compartmentalizing things. Her father had taught her that. His whole life had been sectioned off into small compartments. If it seemed cold, well, that is what you had to do to be one of the best serial killer hunters in the FBI. And she would do it.

She turned on the water and splashed it on her face. She would just have to get Rome to understand that while last night was great, and she definitely wouldn't turn him down if he wanted a repeat, for work they needed to keep it on a professional level. Grabbing a towel she wiped her face off and tried to remind herself why that was so important. Instead, images from the night before came to mind. She'd had sex before. She hadn't been a virgin. But she had never experienced anything like it. Worse, she knew that he had been gentle with her considering his reputation at the club. That was not a full-on submission. She had seen enough of them to know better. It had almost killed her, and he had gone easy on her. He was more than she could handle, that was for sure.

Maria wasn't a fool. She knew part of it was just the image he had of her last night. They were playing roles. Lines could get blurred when you were undercover. She had learned that on her first job. She'd thought she had made a friend in a fellow agent, and he'd just used her to get ahead. Then he'd stopped talking to her. It hadn't been a sexual relationship, but he had been one of few friends she'd made at the FBI. And he had been the last.

"We have work to do, Callahan," Rome said. She jumped at the sound of his voice, but she could hear the amusement in it.

"Bite me, Carino."

He chuckled. "I'm hungry so hurry up."

She grumbled but finished cleaning up and opened the door, expecting to see him there. But he wasn't, and she tried to ignore the disappointment she felt. She grabbed a pair of jeans and shirt and slipped them on. When she walked out into the living room, he was drinking coffee.

"Where did that come from?"

He shrugged. "It was in the fridge." She made a face, and he laughed.

He rose from the table and walked toward her. Damn, she was going to have to get used to the idea that a man she was intimate with was going to see her every day. It was an odd thing.

Always make sure to keep things on a platonic level, girlie. Men will try to use you to get ahead in the FBI. Remember that.

Yeah, remember that. But her father never had to deal with a delicious specimen like Rome Carino. And he had nothing to gain from her. Oh, they could catch the serial killer, and lord knew in Hawaii, that would be huge. It could make his career. But he didn't have anything to do with the FBI. So while working with her helped him, she had a feeling that he didn't look at working with her in those terms. His mind was on finding the killer.

He stopped in front of her, grabbed her by the arms and pulled her closer for a thoroughly arousing kiss. His tongue swept inside, and she couldn't keep that wall built up. It crumpled under his sensual assault.

When he pulled back, both of them were breathing heavily. Her brain had just stopped working. She couldn't even think of a word to say, but apparently Rome had no problems with that.

"Morning again, Maria."

If she hadn't heard the deep need in his voice, she would have been embarrassed by her own reaction.

"Morning again, Rome."

He smiled, satisfaction in his gaze as he released her. "Let's go get a bite to eat. I worked up an appetite last night, as I am sure you did."

"Wait, before we go, we need to come to an understanding."

He raised one eyebrow but said nothing. He still had his hands on her upper arms and it was wreaking havoc with her head.

"We can't let what happen interfere with the investigation."

He nodded, still saying nothing. It was enough to unnerve her and that was odd. Her father had been a quiet man except for when he was telling her what to do. She pushed that thought aside.

"So, it's best when we're out of the bedroom, it stops."

Something she couldn't quite read flashed in his gaze before he hid it behind a mask. "And what does that mean?"

She shrugged, hoping he would take his hands off her, but he didn't let go. It was an odd situation having his hands on her. "I understand what happened is all part of the job."

His eyes turned to ice then. "Really? Do you fuck everyone you work with, or just the undercover assignments?"

His tone lashed out at her. She didn't know how to respond to it. His fingers had tightened on her upper arms, and it was now starting to hurt. She shook herself free then stepped back. "No I don't. After some bad experiences, I don't get involved with other agents."

He studied her for a second. She badly wanted to know what he was thinking, but he kept his expression impassive, not allowing her any hint to what he was thinking.

"So, you don't sleep with everyone."

She closed her eyes as she felt tears prick the back of them. An emotion she couldn't figure out welled up in her chest. When she felt as if she'd gotten herself back under control, she opened her eyes.

"I'm not built to handle this, to handle you. I don't have long relationships for a reason. And I know with an assignment like this, it can blur the lines. I just wanted to make sure that during working hours, it's normal."

Silence filled the air between them, and he said nothing. Dammit, he was starting to make her feel like a specimen again. She'd spent most of her life like that, but with Rome it bothered her more than she wanted to admit.

"Agreed, as long as you understand that if another man touches you while we're involved, I'll tear his arms off and beat him over the head with them."

He said it in such a cheerful voice she didn't catch on to what he said for a second.

"That's barbaric."

He grinned at her. When he did, he looked much younger. His hazel eyes now looked more green than brown, and dammit, the man had a freaking dimple. She couldn't say anything at the moment. Any words of admonition stuck in the back of her throat.

Rome winked. "What can I say, love? You bring out the Neanderthal in me." He grabbed her hand. "Let's go eat."

She opened her mouth, but he just kissed her then. Quick, hot, and it had her yearning for more by the time he pulled away.

"Don't worry about it. Your brain is working without nourishment. That's never a good idea."

She wanted to argue, but she knew he was right. Besides, discussing what happened the night before was too much to handle without a cup of coffee.

"Okay, why don't you show me a cool local place to eat for breakfast?"

. . . . .

Rome ignored the clatter of dishes down the aisle as he watched Maria eat. Good lord, the woman could pack it away. When she had ordered the breakfast sampler, he had thought he would have a little extra to eat. Women rarely ate much around men, but apparently she had no problem eating in front of a man. It was something else he liked about her.

She looked up from her plate and frowned.

"What?"

He shrugged and smiled. Maria was a normal size woman, and he was glad she had a healthy appetite. He hated eating with women who picked at their food.

"Nothing. You seem to have an appetite."

"Well, when I was growing up, you never knew when Dad would stop again. I learned to eat whenever there was a chance. When Big John got it in his head to chase a killer, nothing got in his way."

Apparently not even the health and safety of his daughter, his only child. Rome had always admired her father—still did—but he was starting to get a little pissed on her behalf. What kind of fool dragged a twelve-year-old behind him while chasing scum? You might have to give up something, but family was more important than that.

He brushed aside his aggravation. Getting mad at a dead man when Maria didn't seem to care would be a useless exercise and a waste of energy.

"I'm not complaining about your appetite. In fact, it's nice to have a woman eat a meal I paid for."

She grinned, and his breath caught in his throat again. She was undoing him in simple ways, and she had no idea. After taking a sip of coffee, she glanced around the café.

"Can we talk here?"

He nodded. It was early, and there were very few people in the diner. They had grabbed a corner booth, and no one was around them.

"Did you get those membership rosters?"

He nodded again. "Of course, they're trusting us not to release the names."

She rolled her eyes. "I'll make sure not to mention them when I'm interviewed by Anderson Cooper next week."

"The FBI isn't the best when it comes to discretion, and they have been known to be the morality police."

She snorted. "Yeah, especially Hoover, and he was a man who wore dresses. I'll make sure none of it gets out."

Rome should have known that Maria would have a common sense attitude about the whole thing, He nodded and picked up his fork again. "I don't know if you'll find anything. We checked them out a month ago."

She took another sip of coffee. "Yeah. I was worried about that. We might have someone who isn't a member but stalking them, you know what I mean?"

It was his fear. It was the one reason he thought they hadn't been able to nail anyone down. What if it was a friend of a friend of a friend? That was the way it went sometimes. Worse, the fact that he might know the killer, have had drinks with the bastard…it ate at his gut on a daily basis.

"Dad always said you have to look at the crimes, the way they are handled, to figure out the killer."

"I did take that class off him." He couldn't hide the sarcasm in his voice.

She nodded. "But if it is like we think, if it's someone in

law enforcement, he could be doing things in a way to make us think he's different than he is."

"What do you mean?"

She pursed her lips. "The guy is smart. No doubt about it. So if he is that smart, he could be sending us on chases after a person who doesn't exist."

"He knows the mentality, the FBI playbook? So he does things to throw you off?"

She shrugged. "Could be. Not like there aren't a hundred shows to teach you how to do it, and thousands of sites on the Internet with instructions."

He shook his head. "Someone in that kind of frenzy wouldn't be thinking of that."

She opened her mouth and then her attention went to someone beside him. He looked up and found Jack standing there. Shit. Rome wasn't in the mood to deal with his now-former partner. Jack wasn't a bad guy, but he wasn't someone he wanted to deal with. And not someone he wanted around Maria.

"Hey, Jack. How're you doing?"

Jack was watching Maria with an interest that Rome didn't like. Jack's marriages ended up in the gutter because he cheated on all his women constantly. Jack didn't believe in being faithful. More than once he'd gone after one of Rome's lovers after he'd split. He didn't think it had anything to do with Rome, but that the women might have been vulnerable…and easy.

"Thought I would grab something to eat before I go on over to mediation."

He barely gave Rome any attention.

"Maria, this is Jack Daniels."

Jack tossed him a look of aggravation. He turned back to Maria with a smile. "Jackson Daniels."

She offered Jack a smile that had Rome biting back a growl as something dark and nasty coiled in his gut. Did she have to be so friendly with the idiot? He took a smile as an invitation to sex.

"Nice to meet you," she said with just enough southern accent that she had him blinking. Then he remembered, she had used it the night before.

Jack, damn him, widened his smile. "I can't believe I haven't met you before. I know most of Rome's…friends."

Rome bit back a snarl. "We just met."

"Ah, that explains it. Tourist?"

Maria practically batted her eyelashes at Jack. "Does it show?"

"Not much."

Rome decided he'd heard enough. If he let it go on much further, there was a good chance he would beat up his ex-partner…or blow their cover. At the moment, Rome wasn't all that sure which was worse.

"You might want to order your breakfast or you'll be late. For your divorce proceedings."

Jack shook himself and looked at Rome. It was as if he had just noticed he was there. "Oh, yeah."

"This is your…what? Third?"

"Yeah. And there's my lawyer," Jack nodded toward the door. "It was very nice meeting you, Maria."

"Same here."

He left and headed off to the well-dressed shark who kept punching something into his phone. When Jack was out of earshot, Rome turned around and found Maria smirking at him.

"What?" he asked.

"What was that display for?"

He fought not to fidget, but it was hard. "Jack has a reputation."

One eyebrow rose. "And you don't?"

"I don't."

"Funny, your friend seems to think you do."

He shifted in his seat. "First, he isn't a friend. He's my ex-partner. And second, Jack always thought I had a lot of women, and I don't. Not any more than the next guy."

Her smile widened. "That's not what I heard at the club last night."

"What do you mean by that?"

"Well, the women were all talking about you last night. I mean, the subs do like to compare notes."

He frowned. "There was no one I dated there last night."

She didn't say anything, just kept looking at him over the rim of her coffee cup. He could tell by the way her eyes were sparkling she was messing with him. And she had a right. He knew exactly what he was feeling, and it was jealousy. He hadn't felt this for years, and never this violently. Jack, a harmless pain in the ass, had sent such a rage through him for just flirting with Maria. He was acting like a jackass, and he knew it.

"So, how about we get together this afternoon and work over those names again. We sent them through once, but it wouldn't hurt to look at some of them again."

"And the employees," she added.

"You don't suspect Evan or Micah?"

She shook her head. "I told you I didn't. They both have juvenile records which are sealed, but both of them have walked the straight and narrow, and they haven't been on the mainland in years. Plus, I talked to a former FBI agent who could vouch for their characters…and they both have alibis for the killings. Again, we need to find someone who has some kind of connection to law enforcement. They would have to have intimate knowledge of your investigation and of the FBI's. I just don't see that happening."

He nodded. "I hate to say it, but we better check out the patrol officers. Hawaii has done a lot recruiting the last few years. People from all over."

Something caught her eye again, and Rome followed it. Ashton walked in, a small, timid looking Asian woman on his arm. He turned in the opposite direction of the booth where they sat.

"Well, I didn't expect to see him again so soon," Maria said.

Rome watched as Ashton allowed the woman to slide into the booth before he joined her on the same side. He glanced in their direction and sneered, but then smoothed his features as the woman drew his attention to the menu.

"I guess we can meet up at my house after lunch."

She said it just a little too casually, as if she were trying to hide something.

"Got plans?"

She shrugged. "Just a few things I have to do."

"You got a hot date?"

Her face flushed. "No. Good lord, no. I'm going by Dupree's to have lunch with May."

She looked so cute, sipping her coffee, a bright blue shirt hugging her body and the Hawaiian morning sun streaming in behind her. He should say something, but it was hard to get his tongue to work when it was tied in knots.

"Rome?"

He shook himself out of his stupor. "What?"

"You have a funny look on your face."

Of course he did. He was staring at her, unable to utter a word. "Uh, nothing."

"Okay. I'll talk to the ladies again about the four dead women here. Also, I'll go through the backgrounds on all those women."

He frowned and she nodded. "I agree. We have to tread lightly because we don't want people to think we're persecuting them because of their sexual preferences."

She was gathering up her stuff, as if getting ready to leave. He was trying to think of something else to say. Why? He had work to do, a killer to catch, and he was mooning over a woman. Trying to come up with more conversation. It was a little bit pathetic.

When she noticed him watching her, she opened her mouth to probably ask him what he was looking at her for, but he started slipping out of the booth.

"I gotta get to work."

She took another quick sip of her coffee, stood and reached for the check. He grabbed it up.

"Hey, I'll pay."

"I can pay for breakfast after a date."

She shook her head as she rose from the booth. "It's the FBI's dime."

He snaked his arm around her waist and pulled her against him. He liked the fact that she was tall, that he didn't have to bend down to kiss her mouth. He did just that. Quick, hot, and thoroughly arousing. The dazed look on her face gave him satisfaction.

"I just wanted to make sure you knew that the morning after…and the night before, never has anything to do with the FBI, the case, or work."

She pulled her bottom lip between her teeth, and he gave her another kiss. He guided her to the door, hopeful that he could remember that this was temporary. Still, it was hard to remember when everything, from the night before, to sitting in the diner eating breakfast, felt right.

. . . . .

His heart smacked against his ribs as he looked around the corner. Anger and arousal filled him, and he did not like it. A true Dom wouldn't lose control by just looking at a woman. No emotion could have power over him. Drawing in a few deep breaths, he watched the detective and his newest slut walk out of the diner and down the street. It really had been luck that he had found them there, watched them from the street. The night before told him that the bastard would bring her home. Carino always got women to spread their legs like the sluts they were.

He tried to follow them, but he couldn't keep up without

drawing Carino's attention. They turned a corner that he knew would lead them to a parking garage, probably where Carino had parked. He waited and was irritated when he watched the detective's car zoom out of the garage some moments later. The car sped off in the opposite direction of the HPD. Of course. The slut had left her car behind at the club.

He shivered, his body hot and cold at the same time. Sweat beaded his upper lip as he tried to warm himself up, but he couldn't seem to. He needed to kill again, needed to feel the power of draining life from a woman's body and releasing her to hell where she belong.

He needed to hunt.

Chapter Eight

"You're going over the lists again?" Micah asked as he poured himself a coffee. He held it up as an offer to Rome, and he waved it away. His nerves were already a tangled mess. Adding more caffeine would just make it worse.

"Yeah. We might pick up on someone we didn't before, someone connected to the feds in some way, or having some connection to be able to find out where and when the FBI was showing up. Plus, we're going to go over some of the patrol cops around here."

Micah nodded as he settled in his chair behind his desk. "That sounds like a good idea."

"But?"

Micah shrugged. "This is a 'needle in the haystack' kind of thing. Another thing you'll want to do is look at the patterns in their lives."

"We did that. Nothing connects."

"When I was bounty hunting, one of the things I was good at was looking into people's backgrounds."

The interested look in his friend's eyes told Rome he wanted to help. He could let Micah help a little, but he couldn't let him put his life on the line.

"No. Other than allowing us to use your club for a sting, I don't want you near this."

Micah chuckled. "Oh, I don't want to help. But you need

to go back through their personal lives. Since this is all sexually charged, and all of the women went to the same clubs, you might want to look more into not only who they were involved with, but what particular type. I'm pretty sure the local cops didn't. And from what you said, the first FBI agent fucked the investigation up. I can almost promise you some of those steps were missed."

Rome nodded, mentally adding up everything they had to go over. More than likely Maria had already done it. Knowing her, she already had a long list of things she needed to check and recheck. He couldn't stop the smile when he thought of her looking flushed and happy in bed this morning. She hadn't expected him to tease her. All it made him want to do was tease her more. He had a feeling that there hadn't been a lot of light and happy moments in Agent Callahan's life.

"How was it between you two?"

Rome came out of his musing and looked up at Micah. "What?"

"You practically ran out of here last night. Everyone was talking about it."

That caught his attention. "Everyone?"

"You know, the regulars. You don't normally act like that. You have a reputation for being pretty ice cold in your seduction. Of course you drew some notice when you practically beat your chest like a caveman and dragged her out of here last night.

He said nothing, just stared at his friend.

"I have to say, I am a little confused. You told me it was all just undercover work."

Rome could tell by his friend's tone that he was screwing with him. "You don't say."

Micah nodded then sipped his coffee. "So, I guess your reaction was all part of the ruse?"

Rome said nothing, just kept staring at him.

"Of course, it was good because there are at least half a

dozen men interested in her now. And that'll help with the investigation. They want to know if she lived up to your expectations."

"What the hell does that mean?"

"It isn't like you get too attached to your subs. A lot of these guys are waiting to see how interested you are in her and when she'll be available. You know a good sub is hard to come by."

He felt his eye start to twitch. Just the idea that they were thinking they had a chance at her had his temper soaring. It was irrational and stupid. And, he was sure most people would point out, not very Dom-like.

"And?"

"Well, I'm sure they're just waiting to pick up your leftovers. Especially Ashton. He really has a thing for her. He was trying to pump Dee for info last night."

The idea of that slime touching Maria had Rome grinding his teeth. "If one of them even thinks of touching her, I'll break his fucking hands."

Micah chuckled again. "You're easy."

Irritated with his friend and with himself, Rome stood and started pacing. He didn't know why he was acting like an idiot. He was becoming obsessed. Yes, they had shared something extraordinary, but it wasn't like he hadn't had that connection before with a sub.

As soon as he thought it, he mentally chastised himself. There was nothing normal about what had happened the night before. They had only played a little, and he was already hooked on her. It was a bad thing when he hadn't even gotten a complete submission from her. Hell, they had barely touched the surface. But somehow he felt more linked to her than any other sub before.

"Earth to Romeo."

He shook himself out of his stupor and found Micah staring at him. Rome wanted to cringe at the knowing expression on Micah's face.

"What?" he asked. Hell, he could hear his defensive tone.

"You might want to tone it down a bit."

Rome rolled his shoulders. "You said yourself it caught people's attention. That's the plan."

But even now his gut was churning. He didn't like the idea of men even thinking of her that way. It was the plan. It was reckless and probably a little stupid, but it just might work. Hell, it was working. Being involved with him, the man who was hunting the serial killer, would make an even more enticing catch. How many times had she said that?

"But if you aren't careful, you might end up with too many suspects."

"Especially that damned Ashton. Why do you let him be a member?"

"He paid his dues, and he never gives us a problem."

"Other than fucking with his subs' brains. You know he's an asshole."

Micah nodded. "But he isn't that dangerous. Unless you have some kind of information?"

Rome shrugged. "He's gone after my subs after we split ways."

"As have a lot of the men in here. You're going to have to come up with something better than that." Micah studied him for a moment. "You've never shown any possessiveness before. Not like this."

"I said leave it alone, Ross. If there isn't anything else, I need to get back to the station. I've been running some names through the system, might pick up on something."

"I'll leave it alone as long as you remember, while you might be tied up, figuratively, with Agent Callahan, keep your mind on the job. I'm damned sick of losing people I know and care about."

Rome nodded and walked out of the room. As he jogged down the stairs, he made a mental note to run Ashton's name again. He didn't trust the bastard, and it had more to do with that than Ashton's interest in Maria. They had run his name before, but he decided it would be best to try it one more time. With Maria on the line, he didn't want to take any chances.

. . . . .

"So, how was your night?" May asked. A twinkle in May's eyes told Maria that the woman had heard about her leaving with Rome.

Maria couldn't think of anything to say to the question. They had just sat down at a booth, and she hadn't even had a drink of her soda.

"Uh…" Her mind was blank. Again, she was no good at girl talk. How much did they tell one another?

"Jeez, May, have a heart. Not every woman wants to spill info about their sex life over appetizers." Dee rolled her eyes. "You have to understand she grew up with a horde of men and doesn't know how to act around girls."

Maria shrugged. "I mainly grew up with my dad. Well, and the other FBI agents."

"Your mom?" May asked.

"She died when I was twelve."

May's eyes softened. "Oh, I lost my mom, too, right about the same age."

She didn't offer Maria sympathy, which was best. Talking about her mother, especially the way she died, was something she tried to avoid.

"So it was just you and your dad?" Dee asked.

Maria nodded. "I was homeschooled a lot of the time because I went with him on cases."

There was a long beat of silence and then May opened her mouth. But before she could ask another question, Chris Dupree, the owner of the restaurant, stepped up to the table with their plates. He was a beautiful man with skin the color of rich cocoa.

"Three Kalua Pork Plates," he said, the sound of New Orleans lacing his words. He flashed a smile that was complete with dimples. "I can promise you it's Mo' Betta."

"Thank you," she said as she breathed in the smoky scent of the meat.

"Did you get those schedules done for next week?" May asked as she picked up her fork.

"I'm working on it."

"You better get it done today, or we might have to have another talk."

He chuckled. "Do you remember who owns this restaurant?"

"Do you remember who runs it?" May asked without looking up from her food.

His big, booming laugh echoed through the restaurant. "That's definitely the truth."

When he kept standing there staring at her, Maria didn't know what to say. May leaned over. "He won't leave until you try it and tell him it's the best you've ever had."

She scooped up a huge forkful and took a bite. The moment she did, she hummed. The smoky taste, along with the juiciness of the meat, was wonderful. After she swallowed, she said, "It's the best I've ever had."

"I bet it's the only Kalua pork you've ever had," Chris said.

"Oh, leave her alone. Besides, your soon-to-be ball and chain is here," May said as she tilted her head toward the door.

Chris glanced over his shoulder, and if a man's face could light up anymore, Maria'd never seen it. She felt a small twinge that felt like jealousy. A slightly pregnant blonde was slowly making her way over in their direction.

"I'll see y'all later."

He turned and left and met the woman halfway across the room. He slipped his arm around her waist then led her to the back of the restaurant.

"That's his wife?"

"Soon-to-be wife. They're getting married next month. And they know who you are," Dee said casually.

Maria sat back and frowned at the two women. "That wasn't approved."

"Oh, pooh. The problem is while Chris and Cynthia aren't owners, they're very close to us. We thought it best they know what was going on. They won't be around the club at all right now. Ever since Samantha was killed, Chris has pretty much told Cynthia she couldn't go. They really don't play there much anymore," May said.

"Do you two?"

"I work there of course, so I'm there a lot of nights." There was something in Dee's tone that told Maria that she wasn't being completely truthful.

May took a sip of her drink and then smiled. "Micah has a secret room."

Maria looked at Dee and had to swallow a laugh. The woman worked at a BDSM club, and she was blushing about a secret room. "It isn't a secret room, like most people don't know about it."

Maria sighed. "What kind of secret room?"

Dee's eyes widened. "Oh, nothing like that. It's more like a studio apartment. When they first opened the club, Micah slept there a lot of nights. Most nights, from what he told me."

"And now they go back there and play."

"*May.*" Dee closed her eyes. "Good lord, you don't have a filter on that mouth."

Her friend waved it away. "Our agent here was wondering if she was wrong about you and Micah."

Dee's eyes popped open. "Is that true?"

Maria looked from one woman to another. "No. We checked all of you out. But, I would say that if people knew it was there, it could be a place to hide."

"Ah, well, hard to get in there. Only Cynthia and I have

been in there, other than when Dee and Micah get it on at work."

Dee looked ready to kill her friend, so Maria changed the subject. "I want to talk about the four women."

Both of their expressions sobered. Maria regretted it, regretted that she was the one who had to do this. She had really enjoyed the short interlude, but truthfully, she understood what was at stake. They had to catch this son of a bitch before he killed again.

"No problem. But I'm pretty sure the police and the FBI have been over that," May said.

"What I want is things that might not be covered in that. I know they may have talked to people about their boyfriends, their Doms…anyone they were involved with. But can either of you think of anyone who had issues with them?"

May made a face. "Only one who had an issue with Angie, the second victim, was me. She had a thing for Evan. But I threw Kai at her for a while, and she was satisfied."

"The last time I saw her was up at Ala Moana beach. She was pissed. Oh, man was she pissed," Dee said.

"Can you remember about what?"

"Ticket. She said she got a ticket for speeding, then a fine because her tags had expired. She got in a little scuffle with the police officer, too."

"You know, Devon had an issue, something with a neighbor. She'd made a complaint about the guy who lived above her."

"Was she afraid of him?"

May laughed and a few of the patrons' heads turned in their direction. "Sorry, but you didn't know her. She was small, but she was a black belt."

That caught Maria off guard. "I don't remember that being in the report."

May shrugged. "She didn't hide it. I know most everyone knew she used to compete. She was damned good. That is always why it struck me as odd that she was one of the victims. It made me…"

Maria leaned forward, she couldn't help it. "What?"

"It isn't that important," May said, waving it away.

"No, everything is important. You might even think it isn't that important, but it is. So tell me."

May shrugged. "I figured that the only way she would have been attacked and not prepared was if she knew the guy. She had to have known him."

"I wouldn't want to meet up with her in a dark alley, and I know how to protect myself," Dee said.

Knowing the woman had been on the run from her family for ten years, Maria could just imagine. "So, they both had issues with the police right before that. And we know that Devon could take care of herself in a fight. One way or another, she was surprised."

Maria pulled out her notepad and made a few marks. May leaned over and frowned. "What the heck is that?"

"Shorthand. Or a kind of shorthand. My father made it up. We were the only two who knew it."

"Oh."

"So do you know if Lisa had issues with the police before this?"

"Oh, I don't know. Do you, Dee? Did she mention it?"

Dee shook her head. "She was really a loner. She hooked up, don't get me wrong, but she didn't share a lot about her background. Unless it interfered with work, she didn't tell me anything."

"Do you think it could be the same policeman?" May asked.

Maria thought about it but dismissed it. "Probably not. If it was, it would have been picked up on way before this. But it is a connection outside of the club. Coincidences, no matter how small, are always important."

She finished her notes then set them aside. She looked down at the plate that was still half full of food. "If I keep eating like this, I'll have to go on a fast when I get back to

DC."

"Do you like living there?" May asked.

Maria shrugged. "It's where work is."

"So you don't have someone you live with there, a roommate?"

Maria swallowed the bite of pork. "Nope."

Dee sighed, aggravation easy to hear. "What May is trying to ask is if you have a significant other?"

Maria frowned. "No."

"Oh."

Dee rolled her eyes. "May is a little protective of Rome, just so you know. Probably because he has a crush on her."

"He *had* a crush on me," May said, turning her attention to Maria. "I would say that he definitely doesn't anymore."

Maria wanted to disappear. Just looking at May, she knew the kind of woman Rome usually was attracted to. Petite, exotically beautiful…not something anyone in his or her right mind would call Maria. She pushed that aside. She couldn't think about what Rome liked or didn't like, not right now. Sure they had a night that blew her mind. Hell, her body was getting hot just thinking about it. But it was probably pretty stereotypical for him.

"Are you asking if my intentions are honorable?" Maria asked, hoping that her tone was filled with just enough amusement that she hit the right note.

May studied her for a second, then two, and then her shoulders relaxed. There was something that moved over her face, but she said nothing about it. "Sure. Rome's a big boy, he can handle himself."

"Speaking of which, I need to get going. We're supposed to meet up to go over some of this stuff." She slipped out of the booth. "How much do I owe?"

May shook her head. "On the house, sistah."

"Oh, well…I guess I should get going."

With that she fled the restaurant, ready to get back to the investigation and away from May's probing questions. She didn't want to ask the questions of herself, so she definitely didn't know how to answer May. Maria was pretty sure if she spent too much time thinking about what had happened the night before, she might get too upset thinking that she only had a short time to experience Rome.

. . . . .

"What the hell was that all about, May?" Dee asked.

May was still looking at the door where Maria had escaped. And that was the right word. She had acted as if the dogs of hell were following her out the door.

"She's an odd one."

Dee snorted. "Fine one to talk."

May turned her attention back to Dee. "No, really. Can you imagine having to follow your father around while he hunted up crazy people? That's no life."

"True. But I can't say much about it considering my family." She paused. "You worried about Rome?"

May shook her head. "I was a little worried at first. When you told me his reaction, then what happened last night, I was really concerned. But, I am pretty sure he's safe from her."

"How can you be so sure?"

She thought of the way the woman looked when May talked about Rome. "Did you see the way her face got all dreamy? They only had one night together, and that woman is hooked."

"Well, Rome does have a reputation."

"Yeah, and one of the things is that he never gets really attached to women. From what you told me about last night, he is very attached to Maria. I just don't want to see him go."

"Go where?"

"I worry she might lure him back to the mainland."

Dee snorted. "You always make it sound like a cesspool,

but I seem to remember someone had a very good time in Vegas at her bachelorette party, even if she couldn't remember it when she got home."

May laughed, allowing her worries about Rome to be pushed to the back of her mind. "Well, there are small parts I remember. There was that tattoo parlor Cynthia just had to go to."

. . . . .

Maria spent all afternoon going over her notes. She found eight of the women had some kind of contact with the law. Her eyes were starting to cross, so she set it aside and opened her laptop to work. Not her real work—her paying job—but while she was waiting for Rome, she figured she could get a few words in for the day. As she waited for the laptop to load, she thought about what her father would think about her writing hobby.

She laughed, but there was no joy in it. He would be embarrassed that his little girl saw herself as an aspiring romance writer. Maria would never think of herself as an author. She had no plans to even send the books out. True, it had turned into an obsession, but she figured a shrink would tell her that it was her way of coping. Writing had been the one thing she did that kept her sane while she'd been with her father those last few months. It had been her one outlet. Having to watch the once strong and powerful Big John Callahan wither away and die had been almost too much to bear. Writing had been the one thing she could do to keep herself going.

Since returning to DC after his death, she seemed fixated with getting the word count in for the day. And she was behind since she'd gotten to the island. It had been over a week since she'd had time to sit and write. When she heard the car outside, she frowned. Apparently she wasn't going to get any words in for the day. Rome was already at the door by the time she started shutting down. The knock sounded just as her PC started to completely turn off. She rose and walked to the door, opening it for him.

She had known him for three days, and the impact was still the same. Heat hit her the moment she saw him, her body seemingly responding to the fact that he was there. He cupped her cheek and brushed it with his thumb. Without a word, he kissed her, soft, sweet and just enough to have her curling her toes into the carpet. By the time he pulled away, she was ready to beg for more.

"Hi," he said, his voice soft.

"Hi, yourself."

She stepped away then, because she needed to. Her body was still humming from the simple kiss. Rome had other ideas. He grabbed hold of her hand and walked with her back to the living room.

"How was lunch?"

The question reminded her of the last part of her conversation with Dee and May. She couldn't think about that. That was personal, and the most important thing right now was making sure they caught this bastard.

"Good. One thing I'm checking is that two of the women had altercations with the police before they were killed."

He stopped walking and frowned. "Really? Huh. I'm sort of surprised it wasn't noted in their case file."

"It was. I looked over it when I got back and it was. Different officers, different issues. One was speeding. The other made a complaint about a neighbor. It was noted, but nothing that big because both of the officers in the incidents were cleared."

He pursed his lips. "Still, it's a connection between the women."

"Yeah, and I found six more women who had something in the six months prior to their deaths. Problem is, it doesn't mean just city, but also state and federal, so it's going to take me some time. But it could be the way he found his victims."

"Where he goes hunting?"

She shivered. She couldn't help it. Maria was used to the discussions. She had sat in on a lot of them growing up, but it still chilled her that there were people out there hunting humans. It still felt as if someone were walking over her grave when they said it. Especially in a normal tone of voice. Her father and the other officers always used the same voice to discuss their predators as they did to discuss what to have for dinner.

"Yes. It could be that he's a police dispatcher of some sort."

"I thought we could go out to my house tonight," he said in a voice that sounded casual, but it was almost as if he was trying too hard.

She studied him for a few seconds. "Why?"

"I thought we could eat there, go over some of these cases."

"I thought we'd go to the club tonight."

He shook his head. "That would be suspicious. The idea I would take my new sub to the club right after meeting her...people would wonder."

"Wonder what?"

"They would wonder if I didn't have complete control over you."

She snorted. "Like that's going to happen."

His demeanor changed, his body stiffening. He turned to face her and then slowly backed her up against the wall. He let go of her hands and placed a palm on the wall on each side of her head. She lifted her hands to ward him off, but he had other plans.

"Put your hands against the wall. Do it." His tone was harsh. This was not the soft lover she had met at the door. This was another man, her Dom.

She did it without thinking. Even his tone had changed and with it, her body heated. He was an attractive man, one

100

that any woman would want. All hard muscle and dark, delicious skin. Then there were those hazel eyes that seemed to mesmerize her. But it was the way he spoke when he was being a true Dom that got to her. Even now, her body was warming, her nipples tightening against the cotton fabric of her bra. He leaned his face so close, she could feel his breath on her cheek.

"Let's get one thing straight, Maria. By the time I'm done with you, you're going to be the perfect little sub. You'll know just how to act with your Dom. I'll be the one who gives you the gift of pleasure, the one who makes sure you're begging for it. Don't doubt it."

She swallowed. Just hearing the dark promise in his words had her yearning. Never before had she wanted anything more from a man.

"So next time you want to challenge me like you just did, I will make sure you pay for it." He nuzzled her neck, and she felt the brush of his lips on her pulse point. The feather light kiss had her wanting more, but before she was satisfied, he was pulling away. The satisfied smirk on his face told her that he knew exactly what he'd done to her.

"I think you can suffer until we get to my house."

She frowned at him. His voice had changed, his demeanor also. But before she could ask him, he was walking over to the table by her laptop. "Did you want to save this?"

"What?"

He was looking at the screen. "It's asking if you want to save the document."

Crap. Didn't she shut it down? It had made the shutdown sound. "I'll take care of it." Before he could figure out what it was—or at least she hoped so—she stepped in front of him. The document was there, waiting to be saved. She saved it then shut down the computer. "I'll just grab my purse."

"And an overnight bag. I don't want to have to come back into Honolulu tonight."

She raised one eyebrow and crossed her arms beneath her

breasts. "What happens if I say no?"

He gave her a sardonic look. "I think we just covered that."

Chapter Nine

By the time they were clearing the dishes, Rome was doing his best not to crawl up the wall. It wasn't easy. Not with her in his house. He had a lot of little toys he wanted to use on her, and knowing they were just a few steps away, well, it was almost too much to take. He had been systematically touching her, trying to gain her trust in that area. He'd never known such a jumpy woman. Every little brush of his hand had seemed to get easier for her to take as the evening wore on and harder on him. He winced at the word choice. There was a good chance he would end up passing out from lack of oxygen to his brain.

He set his plate on the counter with a definite clink.

"You don't have to do this," he said, slipping a finger down her arm. She shivered but smiled at him.

"You cooked. Rule in the Callahan house was that the person who cooked didn't clean up." She turned the water on and started rinsing off the plates.

He leaned against the counter and watched her. It scared him how much this seemed normal, as if they had been doing it for years. Standing in the kitchen, the sounds of water hitting the sink, and watching her.

Rome cleared the lump that had formed in his throat. "And I take it you did most of the cooking?"

She chuckled, and he tried not to cross his eyes. God,

even something as simple as a chuckle had him wanting to howl. Worse, it made him think of the way she sounded when she moaned his name. Dammit, where was his control? She was talking about her childhood, and he was thinking about just how much fun it would be to bend her over the counter and take her from behind.

She shook her head. "How very chauvinistic of you, Detective Carino."

"It's just hard to see Big John puttering around the kitchen."

She glanced at him, amusement dancing in her eyes. "My father was an excellent cook. I know how to make a soufflé thanks to him. Mom was one of the worst cooks put on this earth. Her meatloaf was considered a toxic hazard."

She was talking about her father on a personal level, something he had yet to hear from her. The few times she'd mentioned her father, it had been in the context of work.

"Your parents had a good marriage." She looked up at him, surprise lighting her eyes. "I could hear it in your voice."

"They did. There were a lot of people who thought they didn't have a good marriage. But, they...clicked. They were so independent, but when they were together, you could see it. With Dad's job, he was gone a lot, but they never seemed to have anything beyond the usual marital problems. Both of them had high stress jobs but they seemed to make it work."

"Your mother wasn't an FBI agent, right? What did she do?"

"Heart surgeon. She was considered one of the best in the country at the time. Still. You mention Selena Gutierrez Callahan in some circles and they know her name. A lot of her papers are still studied at the top med schools."

He heard the pride in her voice and noted it was different than when she talked about her father. "But you didn't go that way."

She shrugged. "Not my thing. Too icky."

He ignored the fact that she was an FBI agent, and she saw lots of icky things. He wanted to know more about her parents, about the people who raised her. "Then your mother died."

She looked away and put his dish in the dishwasher.

"Maria?"

She looked up at him.

"What happened to your mother?"

She sighed. "They kept it out of the papers, but…one of Dad's old cases. He escaped from a maximum security prison."

"And?"

She didn't say anything at first. He was almost afraid she wouldn't tell him, but he waited and was rewarded. "He broke in the house and killed my mother. After that, Dad was never the same. He always saw it as his fault."

"Where were you?"

"One of the reasons Dad blamed himself. We were at a hockey game. We stayed overnight in Vancouver then came back the next morning. It was something we did a lot because he was gone so much."

"You two found her?"

She nodded. "The next morning. Smythson was waiting for us."

"*Jesus.*" Just the thought of the scene she'd seen at the age of twelve sent chills racing through him. And he knew the Smythson case, knew the man had been a sadistic killer. He raped and tortured his victims before he finally killed them. "Your father killed him?"

"It was him or us. No choice."

She said it matter of factly, and that was probably the only way she could deal with it. Seeing something like that would be horrible for an adult, but for her, it must have been horrific. He didn't really know what to say. As a cop, he had handled all kinds of grief from victims, but this was different. It had never been so personal before. He barely knew her, but he felt the pain of her past as if he had known her at the time. He couldn't even fathom what it must have been like for the two of them. Her father had been a proud man. To have lost his wife in such a way would have been almost too much to handle. Before he could think of something to say, she broke the silence.

"I think we need to cross-check all those officers on the cases. Something might click. And we need to look at Lisa's altercation. It might be a red herring, but you never know."

Her movements were brisk and economical, but he sensed the fragility beneath them. He slid his hand down her spine, and she looked up at him with a smile. It reached her eyes, lighting her up from within. He was beginning to realize that he really didn't understand her. Three days earlier, he had judged her to be cold, but just this little glimpse into her background told him just how fragile she was. The hard exterior was there, but beneath it he knew there was a soft woman lurking.

"Yeah, why don't we do that?"

She turned off the water and walked into the living room, and he followed her. Rome had a strange feeling that he would be doing this for a lot longer than either of them expected.

. . . . .

Maria looked over the next report, then rubbed her eyes. The words were blurring together, and she couldn't seem to make them make sense.

"What's the matter?" Rome asked.

She glanced up at him and then back down at the report. "Just starting to get a headache."

He smiled as he set down his papers and laptop and then slid onto the couch beside her.

"Turn."

106

She realized she'd played into his hands, but she wasn't going to fight it. Not when the reward was so wonderful. He settled his hands on her shoulders and started to rub her aching muscles.

"You sit bent over too much. I bet it has something to do with your height."

She closed her eyes and relaxed fractionally. "How do you know that?"

"I have a younger sister almost as tall as you. When she was younger, she always hunched, but my mom always griped at her about it. When she's tired, like you are, she resorts to it."

Maria's aching muscles relaxed under his ministrations.

"Why don't we take a break?" he asked.

"What kind of break?"

"A hot bath. I've got this huge tub, and you could take advantage of it. Soak away some of these aches."

"What would you be doing?"

He chuckled. "I'll stay out here and work."

That smacked of special treatment, and she could feel her spine stiffen. "That's okay."

He leaned forward to press his mouth on the side of her neck. "Maria, no one doubts you're a top rate agent, at least not me. But you've been working on fumes since you arrived on Oahu. You need to take a moment, gather your thoughts. It might even lead to a breakthrough."

She wanted to fight him. In the years she had been an agent, and basically since her mother died, she had always done her share. It was her way. Her father couldn't handle everything himself, and he'd needed her. She'd had no choice when she entered the FBI. Any kind of slacking on her part would make her stand out in a bad way. She was not the kind of woman who sat by and let others do work. But even as she thought it, she knew she was already losing the battle. Inch by inch, she eased back against him as he spoke.

"Okay. Let me get my toiletry bag."

He stood then held out his hand. She looked at it for a second. She was unaccustomed to such behavior. Rome might be a tough cop and an even tougher Dom, but he had the manners of a gentleman. It was as if he treasured her in some way she couldn't comprehend. She didn't think she would ever get used to him. She took his hand and let him help her up. He brushed his mouth over hers, humming as he did it. The vibrations tickled her lips and sent tiny little pulses of heat dancing through her blood. Then he was moving away.

"I'll start the water. Takes a while to get hot."

She watched him walk away, allowing her gaze to slip down his back. The jeans he'd slipped on earlier were worn and fit like an old ball glove. She sighed, partly because she couldn't figure out how she ended up with such a delicious man, and partly because of his behavior. She knew he had been an infantry sergeant when he was in the Marines. He had fought, killed, and had several shootings under his belt as a cop. Not to mention he liked to order her around. She shivered at the thought and forced herself to get her bag. There was something so wonderful about the makeup of Rome Carino. Just when she thought she knew him, he surprised her. She wasn't so sure she liked it. She found her bag just inside the door where she had left it.

As she walked to the bathroom, she thought of her earlier behavior. She never told anyone about her mother's death. It was just easier to let people think her mother died in some kind of accident or of cancer. She'd learned long ago that allowing people to believe in that was easier than explaining what happened. With Rome, though, she seemed not to have any issues. His silence hadn't hurt. In fact, just the small touch to her back did more than any words of condolences had done in the last sixteen years.

She stepped into the bathroom and realized he wasn't kidding. She hadn't been in there before and was mesmerized by it. Even the bathroom in her house back in the DC area wasn't this wonderful. Light grey ceramic tile on the floor, red accents, a double sink vanity, and then there was the tub. It sat next to a wide ceiling-to-floor window. It was a claw foot and about three times the size of any other she had ever seen.

"Where did you get that?"

He smiled at her, and she tried to keep her heart from falling down at his feet. He had one of those smiles that lit up his whole face, including his eyes. There probably wasn't a woman alive that could resist that smile. To keep herself busy, she placed her bag on the counter.

"It came with the house. It was the one thing that sold me. That and the kitchen."

He was pouring in some kind of oil. It was lightly scented but not flowery, thank goodness. She really hated anything that reminded her of a garden. Instead it was almost masculine in the scent.

"Come here," he said and held out his hand.

She did so without hesitation. Maria saw no reason to resist him. Even if she wanted to, she didn't think she could. She was tired, and with the cozy warmth of the moist heat of the bathroom surrounding her, she allowed her entire body to relax. He tugged on the waistline of her jeans and pulled her in between his legs. She smiled when he slipped the button open and then tugged down the zipper.

"I thought you said you'd go back to work."

He sighed. "I did, didn't I? And if I see you naked, that isn't going to happen."

He looked so unhappy, she couldn't resist touching him. She leaned down and cupped his face in both of her hands and gave him a simple kiss, barely brushing her lips against his. When she pulled back, he looked a little stunned.

"Rome?"

He said nothing as he looked at her. She resisted the urge to fidget, just barely.

"Is there something wrong?"

He shook his head. "No, love, there isn't anything wrong. I'll leave you to your bath." He walked to the door then stopped, looking back at her. "Call if you need anything."

She nodded and watched, perplexed when he shut the door and left her. What was that about? She sighed, knowing she wouldn't be able to figure it out. She didn't know the romantic nature of men. Fighting them, or beside them, that was easy. But trying to understand how their minds worked, that was just not her strong suit—not on this level. Hell, she didn't understand what she was feeling, or how to deal with it. She decided she would be able to think better after a long, hot bath, just as Rome had suggested. She tugged off her clothes and sunk chin deep into the scented water, glad that for once she had followed some good advice.

. . . . .

"Anything going on tonight?" Rome asked Micah over the phone. He could hear the muffled music in the background telling Rome that Micah was up in his office.

"Nope. Actually kind of quiet after your performance last night."

Rome rolled his eyes. "I didn't perform anywhere. I just laid the groundwork to catch someone's attention. Did you have any problems with your employees today? Anyone call in sick?"

"No, like I said, a quiet night. I thought I would see you both here tonight."

He bit down on his irritation. "We'll be there tomorrow night. I figured it would be odd if we showed up tonight."

Micah chuckled. "Yeah. Sure, tell yourself that."

"What the hell is that supposed to mean?"

"You just didn't want anyone looking at your new plaything."

"She isn't a plaything. I thought we went over this earlier

today."

"Oh, there's Evan. I'm talking to Rome."

He heard Evan in the background.

"No, he's pissy because I called Maria a plaything."

He ground his teeth. "That's Agent Callahan."

"And he's now saying I have to call her by her title."

Evan said something else, and Rome felt his face heating again. Dammit, these two were enjoying this too much. Soon the phone was jostled, and the next voice he heard was, of course, Evan's.

"Hey, bra, how's it going?"

He sighed, knowing there was no way out of it. No matter how much he tried to keep himself aloof from the whole group of friends, he couldn't seem to do it. They just ignored him.

"Fine. We're looking over all the women to see if they had any contact with police. We've found eight so far. But if some of them were given warnings, or maybe not even named, this could be hard."

"May wanted you to know that she talked to Lisa's roommate, and she said she did have contact with the police."

Rome sat up. "What happened?"

"Nothing big. Her roommate had a fender bender. It was just a few days before the murder."

"Can you shoot me the info on the roommate?"

"Sure." He said nothing for a second. "So May said you're kind of serious about this Maria."

Rome sighed. "I know you and Micah have moved into the Dr. Phil camp, but I don't think I want to discuss my relationship with you."

"You're right. He is pissy. Did you not get her to submit last night? What?" Micah was talking in the background.

"It was one night, and this is part of the job."

"Be careful what you say, bra. Take it from Micah and me. It only takes one time to know someone is that perfect sub. So you better be ready to fight for her if she is."

111

He shifted in his seat, not wanting to talk about it. Hell, he didn't even want to think about it. Rome was pretty sure if he did, he would end up having a full-blown panic attack.

"Again, I'm not in need of any Dr. Phil advice."

"Just trying to save you some problems." There was some talking in the background. Dammit, they were doing it again. He didn't have the patience for this tonight.

"Anything else?"

"No. I'll get the info on the roommate. Be careful."

With that, Evan hung up. He knew his friends were right, but at the moment, he couldn't deal with what was going on inside of him. It was bad enough that a little kiss from Maria had his heart tripping over itself. Less than a week and he was falling for a woman who was going to leave when the job was over.

He walked to the bathroom and listened at the door. He heard no splashing, so he opened the door to check on her. She was sunk down into the water chin deep, her eyes were closed and her breathing even. Dark circles marred the delicate skin beneath her eyes. She hadn't really had a break since she arrived. He was amazed she hadn't dropped the moment they walked in the door tonight. The time change was bad enough, but burning the candles at both ends could end up messing with you.

She was a contained woman who thought she never showed her emotions to the world at large. Most people probably missed them. In the short time that he had known her, he'd realized that the layers she had draped over her were a shield. Just four days and Rome knew he was easily becoming obsessed with her. He noticed every move, every flicker in her eyes, betraying what she was thinking.

Now, though, she lay sleeping, totally silent, the only movement the rise and fall of her chest. He knew he was in deep. Less than a week with her and he was having problems concentrating at work. His ill behavior wasn't something that he would normally do. He didn't let his personal life interfere with the job. It was one thing he'd learned from his father who'd spent twenty years in the Seattle PD, and it was solidified in his years as a Marine. As soon as Maria popped up on the island, all that training dissolved.

Getting involved with her was probably a mistake. Not like before, not like with Renee. No, this time he knew that Maria wasn't dirty. If anything, she was squeaky clean. Probably her father's doing. Still, this desperate need he felt for her was starting to bother him. He wanted to make her happy, see her smile, and get another simple kiss.

Jesus, he had almost come undone by that little brush of the lips she gave him earlier. It had been the first spontaneous touch from her. It wasn't that she didn't shy away from affection. She seemed to soak it up in a lot of ways. He had noticed the way she snuggled closer to him in bed. And when he did touch her, she seemed surprised by it. That made him want to shower her with it. Of course if he came on too strong, she would definitely shy away. He had a feeling she kept herself separate.

"Are you going to keep staring at me?" she asked, her tone filled with light amusement.

"Maybe I just want to watch you."

Her lips curved, and he felt his heart do a little dance. "Okay, then."

He would have thought she would be kind of shy about her body, but she wasn't. Probably that practical nature her father instilled in her.

When she said nothing else, he found himself searching for something to get her to talk. "I thought you were sleeping."

Opening her eyes, her smile turned into a grin. "I was sort of drifting. You were right, this was a good idea."

He cocked his head. "Did you actually just admit I had a good idea?"

"I never said you didn't have good ideas. You said I had bad ideas."

"Your idea of using yourself as bait is the only thing I disagreed with," he said as he approached the tub and sat on the ledge.

"You would do it. Did do it when you worked vice in Seattle."

He nodded as he trailed his fingers in the water. "This is a little different. I had a lot of backup. We have none."

"This is just allowing us to talk to people. Just the little bit I've done in the last few days has helped. Admit it."

Because she was right, he nodded. "But going to the club does what?"

"Not sure right now. I did hear about Ashton. He likes to pick up women you've had."

"He isn't very successful."

"Yeah, a few of the women said to avoid him. He's not the kind of Dom a new sub would go after. They say he messes with a sub's head. One of the women he was involved with tried to commit suicide."

He raised his eyebrows at that comment. "I can't believe that Micah allowed him to stay a member with that on his record."

"It's all rumor and innuendo. She wasn't a member of the club, and she had issues before then."

She moved, causing the water to slosh against the tub. It brought his attention back to her breasts. Because of the cool air, her nipples were hard. He couldn't resist. He reached out and brushed the back of his fingers against the tips. She shivered.

"The water's getting a little cold, why don't you come out of there?"

He held his hand out, and she took it readily. Her easy compliance had his blood humming. She rose out of the water, and he sighed. Water dripped down her flesh, off her nipples. He helped her out of the tub.

"Stay there."

He grabbed the towel and dried her off. He moved his

hands over her body, his pulse pounding.

By the time she was dry, he was ready to strip off his clothes right there and take her. Hell, his hands were shaking. Not for the first time did he realize he was acting like some green Dom, not truly ready to take on his first sub. She turned him inside out without even trying. And the hell of it was that she didn't realize her power. If or when she did, Rome knew he was going to be in big trouble.

He wanted to set her up on the wide bathroom counter and feast on that sweet little pussy of hers. But he had toys he'd bought her, ones he wanted to use on her and only her. Somehow he pulled himself back from the brink of losing complete control.

"Come on, Maria. Let's have some fun."

Chapter Ten

Maria followed Rome into his bedroom. Every step took considerable effort. From the first, she had known sex with Rome would be different, but this was…beyond what she would have accepted just two weeks earlier. She was naked, walking through his house, following him like she was some kind of slave.

She shook that idea away. It wasn't the way Rome saw her. Being the sub didn't mean he didn't respect her. But this was one thing she wasn't prepared for. She'd never been ashamed of her body, but walking naked through a house with a man wasn't something she did on a regular basis. As she stepped into the room, she had to fight the urge to run screaming. She knew he would push her, and ask things of her that she wasn't sure she could give him. She had done enough research to know that last night, Rome had taken it easy on her. She didn't know if she could do it. It would be harder this time. Rome would push her over the edge, push her farther than she'd been before.

He took her to the bed. "Sit down."

She did as ordered and waited. The silence stretched as he went to his dresser and took out some things. At this angle, she couldn't see what they were and her imagination ran wild with the possibilities. Rumor was that Rome preferred anal sex. Could she do that? She had never done it before, but she had been interested in it. In fact, it was the one thing she thought about during masturbation that sent her over the edge.

He turned to face her, a small smile playing over his lips. She loved when he smiled. It made him look so carefree, so much younger. He had these little crinkles that formed around his eyes that just caused her to sigh. It was then that she noticed the wide paddle he had in his hand. She felt her eyes widen at the sight. Large, wooden, with one side padded with red leather.

"You understand when you became my sub last night that you are now mine to pleasure."

She nodded, unable to tear her gaze away from the paddle. He kept stroking his long fingers over the soft leather. She could remember the way his fingers had skimmed over her flesh with the same kind of delicacy he now showed the paddle. Damp heat gathered in her pussy, and she had to force herself not to squirm. She knew without being told that Rome would punish her for it.

Like that was a deterrent.

"I want to go back over the rules, although you apparently have the 'do not speak unless spoken to' rule down."

She said nothing, her focus on the paddle. Did he intend to use it on her? What a stupid question. Of course he did. There was no reason he would have it out right now if he didn't plan on paddling her. Just the thought of having him spank her had her blood churning. Fear and arousal slipped through her veins as she tried to concentrate on what he was saying.

"Maria, look at me."

It took her a second, but she finally raised her gaze to his. His expression was impassive, but she could already see the heat building in his eyes. His gaze was so intense she could feel it all the way to the soles of her feet. If she'd had to speak at that moment, she would have failed. Maria knew

without trying that words would have escaped her. No man
had ever looked at her like she was the only thing on earth he
ever needed. She was trying hard to ignore the way her heart
trembled as her lungs seized. All her rational thought started
slipping away. For once, she wanted to pretend that this was
for good, forever.

"I am going to test some of your limits tonight. There are
situations that might make you uncomfortable. Don't ever
think that using your safe word is a coward's way out. We all
have boundaries. We all have things that we can't do. This is
all about learning these things to better understand our true
selves. Do you understand?"

She nodded. "Yes."

He stepped closer, slipping his hands over her cheek. As
he continued to cup her face, he leaned down and gave her a
kiss. It wasn't very erotic as kisses went, but it sent sparks of
heat racing through her blood. "Good. Now, I want you to
stand up and turn around. Place your hands on the bed."

She complied but apparently it wasn't enough.

"Spread your legs out further."

When he had her in the spot he wanted her in, he brushed
his hand over the full part of each of her ass cheeks. The
touch was delicate, almost reverent. She really hated to think
she was standing there, naked, her most hated body part on
display. But as he caressed her flesh, those worries dissolved.
No matter how she felt about herself, Rome had some kind of
ability to ignore all her self-doubt. The fact that he affected
her so much in such a short amount of time should worry her.
But as his hands moved over her skin, she couldn't think.

With one last soft touch, he pulled away. Without
warning, the next thing she felt was the hard whack of the
paddle. Pain hit her first and then pleasure eased the ache as
little ripples of heat filtered out over her skin. She curled her
toes into the bare wooden floor.

"Aw, honey, you should see your ass."

His voice had deepened, and it sent a dark thrill through

her. She liked the feeling, the way her flesh heated. She was already wet, had been from the time he touched her. But knowing how much it aroused him added to the excitement.

He gave her another two smacks. Pleasure and pain shifted over her as she felt her knees buckle a bit. He smoothed his hand over her ass, his cool palm almost as arousing as the whacks he'd just given her. Her nipples were hard, her clit throbbing, and hot liquid had moved to her sex. Damn, he had only spanked her, and she was ready to come. She closed her eyes and curled her fingers into the comforter on his bed.

"Are you okay?" he asked.

She nodded. He moved away then, and she wanted to turn around to see what he was doing but kept herself still. He hadn't given her permission, and while the punishment might end up being delicious, there was a part of her not ready to test those boundaries.

"Have you ever been interested in anal sex?"

The quiet question had her body heating. She had read about it and had some rather hot dreams about it. It had been the one thing she had always wanted to try. "Y-yes."

There was a beat of silence. "Have you tried it before?"

"No." The one time she had the courage to suggest it, her lover had been disgusted. Worse, he tried to shame her for her desires.

"Hmm. Part of me likes that. I like that no other man has touched you this way."

He skimmed his finger along the seam that separated her cheeks. Instinctively she tensed but then relaxed as he continued to skim his finger back and forth. The delicate touch put her at ease.

"There is another part of me upset that we have to wait. I can't take you that way until you're prepared. But it doesn't mean we can't have fun."

Dark need unfurled low in her belly at the tantalizing comment. The strange mixture of fear and excitement still pulsed through her. Adding to the anticipation was the fact that she couldn't see what he was doing. She could hear his movements. And she had become tuned into him on a different level. Knowing Rome, he was staying out of her line of sight on purpose. She would be pissed at him if it didn't add to her arousal.

A shiver slipped over her as Rome skimmed his fingers between her cheeks again.

"Get up on the bed, on your hands and knees."

She did as he ordered even though her legs felt a bit wobbly. It wasn't until she was kneeling on the bed that she realized she had done so without hesitation. She didn't even question whether to do it. Lord have mercy, if she was with him much longer, she would do anything he wanted, be anything he needed. Before she could panic about that, Rome stepped up behind her. She was kneeling on the bed, stark naked as Rome continued to stand behind her. Her nipples tightened further as cool air rushed over her skin. Now she had no way to move, except to disobey the order he had given her. He said nothing before she felt the brush of his lips over her rear end. She curled her fingers into the comforter on his bed as she tried to keep herself from moaning too loudly. Still, a small moan slipped out before she could stop it.

"You're still trying to hide your pleasure from me, and I don't like it."

There was admonition in his voice. Why did she find that so exciting? She had always been the girl that did all things the right way. Now, for some reason, Rome had brought out the bad girl in her. She wanted to be punished.

He slipped between her legs and set his mouth against her thigh. Slowly he kissed his way up to her pussy. She was wet, dripping with arousal even though he had barely touched her. He skimmed his tongue along her slit, but just enough to tease, to tempt. Before she could gain much pleasure, he was moving away. She closed her eyes and tried to calm her racing heart.

He slipped off the bed, leaving her there on all fours, as if on display. He said nothing, but she heard the noise of his movements as he undressed. She closed her eyes, imagining the hard body that she'd had the pleasure to touch.

He moved to the side of the bed and smiled at her as she looked at him.

"I think you need a little more instruction on how to behave. I know that we're just starting, but you need to learn that in the end, you are under my power."

There was a part of her that hated hearing that. It went against everything she had been taught by her father and later the FBI. But now it was different. In here, for some reason, it felt right.

She watched as he wrapped his hand around his erection. Up and down, his hand moved, and she couldn't help licking her lips. His chuckle broke her concentration.

"You want a taste, Maria?"

His voice rolled over her name, and she could have easily died there. Never had a man sounded so in tune with her before this.

She nodded.

He released his cock and slipped onto the bed, working his head down between her legs so that his cock was in the perfect position.

"Take me in your mouth,"

She didn't have to be told twice. Maria leaned down, wrapped her hand around his cock and took him in her mouth. The salty taste of his pre-come hit her first. God, he was delicious. She moaned against his cock, and he groaned.

"That's right, baby, like that."

He was moving his hips in rhythm with her. She barely paid attention to his movements until she felt his finger slipping into her anus. He must have coated it with some kind of gel. Before she could tense, he pulled her pussy down to his mouth. Now there was no delicate touch. This time his tongue surged into her pussy, and she moaned. At the same time, he started moving his finger in and out of her ass.

God, nothing had ever felt so...decadent. He worked her over, taking her clit between his teeth as he added another finger to her ass. She could feel her orgasm coming as she pulled his cock further into her mouth, and she used her hand on him at the same time. Amazingly, he grew harder, and she was sure he was close to losing himself. She wanted him to do that. She wanted to have him come in her mouth, feel it as it filled her.

But Rome had other ideas. He started eating her pussy in earnest, teasing, and then sucking her clit over and over. Soon the need he'd built swelled inside of her. Even as she continued to work his cock in and out of her mouth, her body started to shake. She didn't know if she could stop it, so she felt better when he gave her permission.

"Come for me, Maria. Do it this one time. Come on."

He muttered against her sex, his heated breath filling her as something so tight exploded. She convulsed as the floodgates crumbled under his assault.

Before she had recovered, he pulled away from her. She almost collapsed and would have if he hadn't caught her hips. She was still shaking with the last remnants of her orgasm when he started to work an anal plug into her ass. He didn't warn her, and she immediately tensed again.

"Take a deep breath and let it out slowly. This isn't any bigger than my two fingers."

Normally she would have snorted, but she heard the thread of need in his voice. He was barely keeping himself in check. She did as he ordered, and soon he had the plug in her. He spread her legs apart, grabbed hold of her hips and thrust into her in one hard movement.

God, she was so full. With the plug in her ass and his cock filling her pussy, she felt ready to burst. At first it almost overwhelmed her, but as he started moving in and out of her, the need rose again. In moments, she was hurtling into another orgasm.

But he wasn't done.

He smacked her ass as he continued to thrust in and out of her. Before she could recover from the second orgasm, she fell into another one. This time she sobbed out his name, unable to control herself. She gave into the pleasure he gave her. When she came for the fourth and final time, he came with her, thrusting into her one more hard time and groaning her name as they both lost themselves to pleasure.

. . . . .

Hours later, in the dead of night, Maria came awake with a start. Her heart felt as if it would jump out of her chest.

"Hey," Rome said, pulling himself up to a sitting position beside her. "Are you okay?"

She drew in a shaking breath and tried to calm her racing pulse. "Yeah, just a bad dream, I guess."

He rubbed his hand down her arm. "What was it about?"

She shook her head, knowing she would never remember what brought the mini-panic attack on. "I have no idea."

She tried to pull away, but he held onto her. The panic swelled. She needed some separation. Her attempt was thwarted by the big lug of man in the bed with her. He pulled her against his chest and then reclined back in bed. She had no choice other than to lay her head on chest.

"Tell me about it."

His chest rumbled against her ear.

"Just a little panic attack, or at least that's what I call them."

He said nothing, just slipped his fingers up and down her spine.

"Well?"

"Well what?' he asked, his voice patient.

She sat up then, and he let her. He had no expression on

his face. And he didn't look like he was ready to kick her out of the bed.

"Aren't you going to ask me why I'm having panic attacks?"

"First of all, you aren't." She opened her mouth, but he ignored her. "What you had was a bad dream. You've been under a lot of stress."

She let loose a breath she didn't know she was holding. She hadn't told anyone about the dreams, her worries. It had been less than a week, but she felt comfortable enough to tell Rome just what she felt.

"On top of it, we didn't use any protection. I'm not usually so careless."

"I'm on the pill, and I know both of us have been tested," she said, but she hadn't even realized he hadn't.

"If there is a problem, you will let me know."

It wasn't a question, or even a demand—just a statement of fact.

"Now," he said. "Tell me how you're feeling."

She almost said nothing. It would be easy to resist the need to share, to let another human being know what she was feeling. It made her vulnerable, and she didn't like it. But for once she ignored her instincts. "I feel like I'm being crushed."

He nodded in understanding. "I know the feeling. You know about me leaving Seattle, right?"

"Yes. Your partner…"

"Was as dirty as a sewer rat. Yeah." He sighed. "I should have known."

"You were cleared."

"Yeah, but for months afterward, I had insomnia. Mainly because I kept going back into that warehouse where I caught her…and she gave me no choice but to shoot her."

"That's tough." And now that she'd said it, she realized how stupid it sounded. It was beyond tough. Your partner was the one person on Earth you were supposed to trust.

More than even your family.

"It was worse. We were sleeping together. It started innocently enough, being undercover the way we were, but in the end, it screwed with my thinking. I doubted myself."

It got worse. Now her worries seemed so small compared to that. And she wondered if that was the reason people said he would never settle down. More than one person had told her Romeo Carino would never settle for one woman. He would have a sub for a while and then they would part ways.

"So, tell me what gives you nightmares."

"Nothing," she said and started to look away. He grabbed her chin and forced her to look at him.

"Tell me."

"Everything. Dad dying. It was tough. I moved back in with him after the final diagnosis. He didn't want to die in a hospital."

"Does any of it have to do with the bullet wound in your shoulder?"

For a moment, she couldn't think of what he was talking about. Then she remembered her rookie year.

"Naw, that happened a few years ago during a bust. It hurt like hell, but wasn't much."

He nodded. "So what else?"

She sighed. "Just all of it. There are a lot of times I wonder if I was cut out to be an FBI agent."

The moment she said the words, she wanted to call them back. She glanced at Rome to see what his reaction was.

"Why?"

"Why? I just don't feel… It's hard for me to describe. But at first I loved it. Loved the fact that I was so good at something."

"You are one of the best agents I've met."

Maria couldn't stop the warmth that filled her chest at the thought. "Really?"

He nodded. "You're smart, and you know a lot about the FBI, probably thanks to your father. But most of all, you're open to other ideas. One of the big mistakes of the FBI, and one reason I decided not to apply, was that they looked at everything in the federal way. One way, never open to other ideas. If you did, you went against the grain. I'd had enough of that in the military."

"You thought about applying?"

He nodded. "After meeting your father, I definitely thought about it. But it wasn't for me."

She snorted. "You would've left before the end of the first year. Not sure your Dom could handle working there."

He smiled, a flash of white in the darkness, and she could feel her heart turn over. Lord, she had it bad for a man when just his smile had her turning to goo inside.

"So what would you do if you weren't in the FBI?" he asked.

She shrugged. "Not sure, really. It's all I've trained for. I guess I like the idea of writing."

His eyebrows rose at that admission, and she tried not to get defensive, but it was hard.

"Like books your father wrote?"

She shook her head. "No. Fiction…more romantic suspense."

He didn't say anything, and she looked away as her face heated. She had never told another living soul that she was writing, except an old lover, and she would never admit to writing romance. Who would expect her to? She definitely hadn't.

"Not like it's anything important. It was just something I did while my father was ill. It was an easy way to escape."

"Don't do that."

"What?"

He shook his head. "It was important, even if you don't do it anymore. It's something that is part of you, and you should never belittle it. Your father's illness had to be tough. I take it you weren't involved with anyone romantically?"

She shook her head, not wanting to admit to him this was

the deepest relationship she'd had with a man. She had never been able to let go the way she did with him. To be close to thirty years old and not able to say she'd had any kind of serious romantic relationship was sad.

"It was what you needed...need." He let one eyebrow rise as if daring her to deny the fact she still wrote. "Whether you do it for just you, or if you have aspirations of being a published author, it is part of you, part of what makes you Maria. What I went through in Seattle with my old partner, it sucked. Fuck, it was the worst thing I have ever been through. Probably because it was the double whammy of a personal and professional fuck up. But I wouldn't change it."

"Really?" she asked, unable to keep the skepticism out of her voice.

"Really. I learned about BDSM because of that situation. I lost complete control of my life there, and I needed something else, knew I was missing it. So, no, I can't say that I would change it. During the process, hell yeah. Nothing like being treated like a leper by people who used to respect you. Worse, the pitying looks from people when they know not only that your career is off course, but you let your dick do the thinking. But, as I said, I found what I needed in the bedroom, and it helped me get back in control of my entire life."

His fervent words rang true, and she could see it in his expression.

"Don't belittle a part of you that is apparently important. It helped you get through a tough time, and it made you even tougher, I bet."

Maria nodded, unable to look away from him. He slipped his hand up to cup her face. His eyes softened.

"Why can't you see that all these things make up one wonderful, sexy woman?"

She blinked, trying to hold back the tears that were now stinging the backs of her eyes. She shook her head. "You don't know me, not really. Admit it."

He nodded. "I do. You're amazing, and until you accept that, you'll never be truly happy."

He was undoing her in small degrees. Didn't he know that this would leave her shattered? She couldn't take anymore, but instead of running away like she usually did, she leaned down and pressed her mouth against his. The warmth of him, the special musky, sensual scent of him, surrounded her as he slipped his arms around her and pulled her down on the bed with him. She didn't want to think or talk anymore, and apparently he sensed it. He took her then, hot, fast, and hard and allowed her to lose herself and forget the worries, even if for a little while.

· · · · ·

The man they called The Dom studied the front of Rough 'n Ready. Fuck. The bastard wasn't coming tonight. He should have known Carino wouldn't make it two nights in a row. But since he'd seen him with his new slut, The Dom was sure Carino would want to show her off.

Another group of giggling women walked up to the front of the club. Sluts. Of course, they were turned away. So many of them willing to play in the rooms of the club, but there was a hefty price tag for joining. If a woman had the money, she could spread her legs for any bastard who thought himself a Dom. There weren't that many.

With disgust, he turned on his car and headed home. He knew where Carino lived and had actually drove past there a few times. But it was best not to tempt fate too much. Fate had made sure he had come to Hawaii to go up against a hotshot like Carino. Seriously, none of the other departments had even bothered him the way Carino did.

But by the end of his time in Hawaii, he would teach Carino just who the true Dom was.

Chapter Eleven

"Rome," someone yelled behind him.

He turned and looked down the hall at the HPD and saw Amy Walsh, a former girlfriend. She was hurrying toward him with a smile. As usual, Amy threw herself at him leaving him no choice but to catch her.

Blonde hair, blue-eyed, and petite, she had a sweet and open disposition. More than once people had referred to the massage therapist as a fairy. All she was missing was the little outfit and the wings.

"What are you doing here?" he asked as he set her back on her feet.

"Gave a friend a ride. He had an appointment here, so I thought I would stop by and say hey."

"You're looking good." And it was true. She had been his longest relationship since moving to Hawaii, a little over three months. She had wanted more and he hadn't, but they had parted on good terms.

"Thank you, as are you." She stood back and looked at him. "I've been hearing rumors from my friends."

"And what would those rumors be?"

She gave him one of her cheeky grins. He had always felt a stirring of heat when he saw them but now, nothing.

"There was a lot of chatter last night at the club that you'd met a new woman and that you were very infatuated. I was hoping to meet her, make sure she's up to my standards."

He couldn't stop the smile that curled his lips or the little spike in his heartbeat at the thought of Maria. Especially the way he'd left her that morning. She'd been so sweet, cuddled in his bed. He had wanted nothing more than to crawl back into bed with her and snuggle the day away.

"Ah, so they were right. I heard she's from the mainland."

"Yeah, here for a few weeks on vacation."

"I went by the club to see you last night. Was sort of surprised you weren't there with this new mystery woman."

"We decided to stay in."

She studied him for a moment and then her smile widened. "It looks good on you."

"Looks good on me? What are you talking about? Have you been smoking any of the White Sage? I knew that stuff was pot."

She laughed. "No it isn't, and you know it. You know I use it to cleanse an area before I give Reiki. Being infatuated, maybe a little in love. It suits you."

He scoffed, trying desperately to fight the worry that had been in his head all day. If he didn't admit it to himself, maybe he could keep himself from falling in love. "I just met the woman."

"You were always a 'settle down' kind of guy, but I figured that you couldn't until you found the right one."

He rolled his eyes. "Listen, I don't need any of your 'woo woo' stuff today. I got a nasty case that is getting worse by the day."

She sobered at the mention of the killings. "Everyone is pretty spooked out there."

"You need to be careful. Even being at the club isn't safe. Don't go off—"

"Oh, God, you sound like my brother. We have already moved on if you are talking to me like that."

130

"I'm worried about you."

"I'm fine. I'm settled."

Something in the way she said it caught his attention. "You've met someone."

When she smiled, it was bright, and it was full of newfound love. "Yes. I have."

He was happy for her, but there was a little niggle of doubt in the back of his mind. "This guy, did you meet him at Rough 'n Ready?"

She shook her head. "No. I'm not ready for you to meet him, but I promise he's trustworthy."

Something in his gut was bothering him. Something that he knew without a doubt wasn't jealousy. "Just because he's a cop doesn't mean he's trustworthy in the dating department."

"Oh, now you really do sound like my brother. Worse, you sound like my father. You know I'm a good judge of character. I dated you for a while."

"That's not proof."

She leaned up and kissed his cheek. "You were always too hard on yourself. When are you going to accept that you're one of the good guys?"

He shook his head and opened his mouth to try to gain a name from her, but she stopped him by pressing her fingers against his mouth.

"Stop. I'll give you a call as soon as I'm ready."

She gave him another kiss on the cheek and then slipped out of the conference room. He stood there for a while, fighting the need to follow her. There was something off about this, something that stuck in his gut. He was about to do that when his cell rang. He recognized Maria's number immediately.

"Hey."

"Hey, I got the info on the other women. Every one of them had some kind of altercation with police in the six months leading up to their murders."

Irritated, he bit back a curse. "I can't believe they didn't figure that out before now. I can't believe I missed it."

"Not easy to find. Not all of them ended up in the permanent files, and not all of them had the dealings in their own city. None of them were arrested for anything, though. Nothing that would raise a red flag."

"But something should have told us."

"Yeah, because the FBI and the HPD are both perfect and never make mistakes." He could hear the laughter in her voice.

"I thought you'd be pissed."

"I am. I should have caught it. I was looking at the big picture, so it was easier than say, well, you. Your main objective is to catch the guy killing your residents. "

"So what's the plan now?" he asked as he saw his chief walk by and motion for him to come to a meeting.

"We need to go back to the club. Hiding in your house isn't going to cut it."

Rome knew that. The best way to get the killer's attention would be to attend the club nightly. It was asinine, but he didn't want another man looking at her. It wasn't as if he had some kind of claim to her, but taking her to the club just didn't sit well with him. He could lie to other people and say it was the danger of the situation, but deep in his gut, though, he knew it wasn't true.

"Rome?"

Her voice brought him back to earth, out of his musings. "Okay. We'll go tonight. I gotta go to a meeting and then I'll be able to break away."

After hanging up with her, he headed off to the department meeting, his mind still on the night ahead. His cop instincts knew Maria's plan would work, and soon. Their guy knew a lot about them, about every case. He would know Rome was investigating and that he was involved with a sub. More than likely, he was casing Rough 'n Ready looking for his next woman. With Maria in the crosshairs, there was a good chance he would zero in on her.

Rome just hoped he didn't lose his sanity or his focus on the case. He didn't want another mistake like before. Of course, having an agent as good as Maria would definitely keep things squeaky clean. The investigation would probably not be a problem.

His heart, now that could be a major problem. Amy was right. They all were. He was falling for Maria, and hard. He knew it was more than her looks. She was perfect for him in that department, but there was something else, that elusive vulnerability he saw last night…it made him want to risk loving again. He doubted she showed many people that side of her. The fact that she did so for him made him feel special.

Jesus, he had to get a grip on his emotions. Or he would be talking to Evan and Micah like they were on an episode of Dr. Phil.

"Carino, get your ass in here," the captain yelled.

All worries about Maria and what would actually come of their relationship faded to the background as he hurried into the captain's office.

. . . . .

Three nights later, they were at the club again, and Rome was getting antsy. The case was getting under his skin. There hadn't been a peep out of their guy in days. Worse, he was really having a hard time being at the club every night with Maria.

She did nothing more than accompany him to the club. She did not flirt and behaved like the perfect sub. Rome, though, was ready to beat the living hell out of anyone who looked their way. He couldn't help the need to touch Maria. He wanted everyone to know who she belonged to. In all his years as a Dom, he had never been so territorial. The double-edged sword was that every time he touched Marie, his frustration rose. Just being this close had his libido running hard.

"Do you want anything to drink?" Maria asked. She had to lean closer, her body rubbing up against his. Her scent captured him, as did the heat of her body. Just thinking that reminded him of the way it felt to slide into that tight little pussy of hers. Nothing had ever felt so right as when he was inside of her.

"Rome?"

He drew himself back from the edge.

"I'll take a soda."

She gave him a look, but there was no way either of them would drink. Even after going over all the information they had, there didn't seem to be any interest from anyone. Not over the top, like someone who might be killing girls would. The sexual tension mixed in with the tension of the case had him ready to scream. Hell, they'd made love before coming out, and he wanted her again.

"Maybe he's laying low, someone who stalks but doesn't talk to you."

He nodded as he scanned the floor again. It was crowded, even for a Friday night.

"You're looking too much like a cop."

He frowned at her. "I am a cop."

She sighed and tugged on his collar until he leaned down. "You're supposed to be on a date with a woman you can't keep your hands off of."

She smiled when she said it, and he knew she was trying to lighten the mood. Especially his. He'd had a bad day at work with his normal work, then dealing with this case. It was starting to give him an ulcer.

"I just don't know what to do," he said, his tone filled with aggravation.

"How about have your drink and wait? It's all we can do. Other than look into backgrounds."

His phone rang, and when he pulled it out, he saw the

dispatch number. He knew it wasn't good.

"Yeah, Carino here."

"We have a woman, dead over in Hawaii Kai."

"Okay, I'm on my way."

He turned it off and slipped the phone back in its holder. She was looking at him expectantly. "They found a girl. Not sure if it's one of the killer's."

Maria nodded, and when she didn't move, he leaned down, caging her in by placing a hand on either side of her on the bar. "You can come."

She shook her head, regret filling her eyes. Knowing the kind of investigator she was, he knew it was probably killing her not to go. "If it is linked, it would be odd if you brought your...friend."

He sighed, knowing she was right. And she was safe enough at the club. That he knew. But there was something that told him not to leave her alone. He glanced around the room, but there wasn't anyone really watching them. They'd garnered a lot of attention when they'd returned, mainly because she was half naked, but he knew that it was normal.

"It might give us an opening."

"I don't like it."

"Yeah, I get that. Go to work, Carino."

He chuckled as he leaned in and gave her a kiss. She wasn't expecting it, and why should she? They had shown some affection in public, but this seemed more normal, as if he were her boyfriend leaving her behind for the job. It was a simple kiss, barely a brush of his mouth over hers. But the warmth of her breath against his flesh sent a wave of heat sparking through his blood. Her bemused expression made him feel a little bit better about leaving her behind.

"You got the key to my place?"

"Yes," she said with just a little bit of sarcasm. And why not? He was acting like an idiot.

"I'll call."

She nodded, and he turned to walk away. As he made his

way through the club, he could feel the stares, knew that some of the men would move in on her. He told himself she could take care of herself.

"Hey, what's up?' Micah asked him at the door.

"Gotta call."

"Someone we know?"

He shook his head. "Not sure. But they find a single woman, possible rape and murder, they know to call me now. I told Maria I'd call as soon as I knew." He looked back to see her talking with Dee, both of them perfectly safe.

"I'll keep an eye out for your lady."

He glanced at Micah. "Thanks. And she'll need a ride home if I can't get away."

Micah nodded. "It might give her a chance to get chatted up with you gone. You tend to give off the 'pit bull guarding the henhouse' feeling around her."

He sighed. "Just make sure she's safe."

He glanced one more time at her. She smiled at him and waved, giving the idea that she was just a tourist there for fun for anyone watching. Then he turned and left, his mind on the work ahead, but his worries on the woman he had just left behind.

. . . . .

"Anyone sitting here," a deep, Australian accented voice said from beside her. She turned and at first couldn't think.

A tall, blond god stood beside her. His skin was dark, as if he spent a lot of time out in the sun. He had one of those strong jaws, and from what she could see, a body that would make a nun want to sin. His icy blue eyes were oddly mesmerizing. Good lord, what did they do? Go out and find every hot nationality there was in the world and bring one guy into Rough 'n Ready from each continent?

"Miss?"

136

She shook her head. "Sorry. Not used to the time change even after close to a week. Seat's free."

He nodded and slipped onto the stool.

"Drinking water?"

She nodded.

"Planning on a little play?"

She glanced at him out of the corner of her eye. "No, since my date is gone."

"Doesn't mean you can't have a little bit of fun before he returns."

She couldn't believe his audacity, but when she turned to face him, she couldn't help but return the smile he offered her. He was gorgeous, that's for sure, and definitely dangerous. But he had one of those little boy smiles that told you he got just what he wanted from women.

"I have a feeling Rome wouldn't be too happy."

"Hmm."

"Hey, Eli, back on the island for a bit?" Dee asked.

He smiled at her. "Yeah. Just the weekend."

"You flew all the way here from Australia for the weekend?" Maria asked.

He laughed. "No, love. I live on the Big Island."

She nodded and took a sip of water.

"I'll take a soda, Dee." His eyes twinkled as he settled his elbows on the bar. "You're looking especially fine this evening."

Dee laughed and shook her head. "I thought you learned last time not to flirt with me."

"No one will ever tell me that flirting with a woman is dangerous."

"Maria, meet Elias St John."

"Nice to meet you, Maria. Did you just move here?"

She shook her head. "Just visiting."

Dee gave St John his change. "Thanks, love. Have you seen Isabella? I was supposed to meet up with her tonight."

Dee frowned. "Bella Sullivan?"

He nodded.

"No, sorry."

She moved down the bar to a new customer.

"So, we're both drinking non-alcoholic beverages and are free for the evening."

She laughed. "First of all, Rome got called to work, so I'm not really free for the evening. You were chatting me up before you even knew your date had left you out to dry."

A flash of something she couldn't discern brightened his eyes before he tamped down on it. It had been hot and lethal. She knew without a doubt this was a man you didn't mess with. He might let everyone think he was just a laid back kind of guy, but he wasn't. There wasn't a doubt in her mind that this man could be deadly when he wanted to be.

"It's odd, that."

"That she stood you up?" she asked lightly. He nodded. "Happens all the time."

He threw his head back and laughed. People turned and looked at them.

"Sorry, that was a right good joke. Yes, it happens to other people, not me."

"Let me guess? No one ever calls you modest?"

"Nope. But then, I don't see a reason to."

His gaze stuck on someone behind her. She turned around and noticed a tall brunette watching them. He refocused on Maria. "So I take it the answer is still no?"

She nodded.

"Well, I'm off for the hunt."

The way he said it sent a chill of ice slicing through her blood. She fought the shiver that sliced through her at the words. With considerable effort, she summoned up a smile.

"Have fun."

He offered her that boyish grin. "I always do, love."

He sauntered off, his gaze on the rather tall woman with the long, dark hair.

"He's not in here that much. He runs a ranch on the Big

Island."

She glanced at Dee and nodded. "There was just something there that bothered me."

"What?"

She shrugged. "Not sure. I'll check him out, though. Shouldn't be too hard to find stuff on him."

"As I live and breathe, Maria Callahan in Rough 'n Ready."

She turned toward the deep, southern voice and swallowed. Her old lover, Malachai Dupree, stood inches behind her, a big smile on his face.

Well, crap. Now she really *was* in trouble.

Chapter Twelve

By the time Rome made it to the scene, something prickled at the base of Rome's spine. There was something wrong. As he made his way up the walkway to the house, he realized it was early in the evening. None of the other killings happened this early. It was usually the dead of night that they found the victim. This was a residence in a pretty decent part of Honolulu. That fact alone had his gut churning.

When he walked up to the crime scene, he was greeted by a patrol officer. Rome showed his badge.

"Detective Carino."

The young officer nodded. "She was found by her mother."

He glanced over at a sobbing woman. A female officer was talking to her. Rome had a really strong gut feeling this wasn't The Dom. It felt wrong, very wrong. Just the fact that the woman had been found in her home should have been the biggest clue. Their killer liked to dump them in the worst parts of town to humiliate them. The moment he walked in, he realized he'd been right. The living room was filled with blood. It was splattered over the walls. The smell of it tinged the air.

"Do you know why I was called?" he asked.

The officer shrugged. "When it was called in, your name was attached to it. Someone did it."

Rome nodded as he saw Detective Sawyer walking up the drive.

"Carino, what are you doing here?"

"My name was attached to it for some reason."

Sawyer frowned. "I have no idea why. We know the ex did this. Or we think he did."

He nodded and started back to his car. Then he stopped and looked back at the house.

"What was the woman's name?"

"Sara Michaels."

He knew the name, knew she was a member of the club, but knew that for once, this was a coincidence.

Still, something nagged the back of his mind, something he knew he was missing again. He was back in his car and dialing Maria's number before he even realized it was now a reflex. Done with work, call Maria.

"Hey, was it one?" she asked before even saying hello. Just hearing her voice had his nerves settling, his worries dissolving.

"No, apparently the woman was in a bad situation with her ex. He's their prime suspect. Are you still at the club?"

"No. I'm on my way back to the house."

"Okay, I'll head back to Honolulu—"

"No, I'm on my way to your house. Malach is taking me there."

He paused. The name was familiar, but it wasn't someone he knew directly. Then it hit him, Malachai Dupree, Chris' brother. He'd met him at Jocelyn and Kai's wedding. "Why didn't you wait for me?"

There was a beat of silence. "I know Malachai. Personally."

Shit, an old boyfriend? Of all things. And that was suspicious. "He found you?"

"We ran into each other. I thought it best to get away from the club to explain so we didn't blow my cover."

"Okay, be there in a few."

"Bye, Rome."

He was irritated, he thought as he drove up Like Like Highway. Worse, he knew why. She was breeching protocol. It was completely out of character for her, and it could endanger the mission. And all because of some damned ex-boyfriend. A Navy Seal ex-boyfriend, in fact. Damned if that didn't piss him off.

When he had been introduced to Malachai at the wedding, he'd seemed a nice enough guy. Women had been slobbering on him, but that was normal for a Seal. The thought that he had been one of Maria's ex-lovers had Rome grinding his teeth. She didn't mention she knew Dupree. It wasn't like they had long conversations about their old lovers, but with the connection, Rome wondered why she didn't say anything.

He pulled back from the idea of trying to kill a Seal, a man trained to kill with his bare hands. But the thing that was starting to bother him was that Maria had a past. He knew she wasn't that experienced, and he never looked down on a woman for her past. But right now, he wanted to beat the holy living hell out of Dupree.

It was worse than when they ran into Jack a few days ago. Now he could feel the slap of anger mixed in with the jealousy. What the hell was he doing? He wasn't a Dom that expected his sub not to have male friends or a past. And he never expected to control their every movement. That wasn't a Dom/sub relationship in his mind. That was a slave/owner and so not his thing.

Still, there was a part of him who thought maybe that was what he should be doing. He should demand that she not have any contact with any men. Which would make both of their jobs difficult and enough to scare the hell out of him.

Irritated with himself and with the woman causing these feelings, Rome punched the gas and sped home. The sooner he saw her, the better he would feel.

. . . . .

"So, you're here working the case?" Malachai asked.

She nodded. "Yeah, I talked them into letting me come over."

He snorted. "Like that was a hard decision. You're one of the best agents they have in their DC office. And that has nothing to do with your father."

"Tell some of them that. But this way I think I'll prove them all wrong."

Malachai frowned. "I don't like it though. Putting yourself out there as bait? Not good. You're sure this Carino guy is good?"

She gave him a sardonic smile. "Do you think I'd work with him if he wasn't?"

He chuckled. "You have before."

She shrugged. "I trust him. Plus he has good cop instincts."

Mal opened his mouth, but the flash of lights told her that Rome had made it back. The door opened just a few moments later.

"Hey, Maria." He walked straight to her and pulled her in for a thoroughly devastating kiss. It was quick, hot, and it made everything in her body pulse.

"Hey, yourself," she said, when she gained her sense. "Mal, this is Rome Carino. Rome this is—"

"We met at Jocelyn's wedding," Rome said as he tucked her close to him. She frowned at him and fought the urge to wiggle away. Something about his expression told her that he wouldn't like it, and he definitely would make a scene.

"Yeah, I remember now. You're the cop who was in charge of May's case."

Rome nodded. Neither of them said anything. Rome kept her locked next to him, and Mal crossed his arms over his massive chest. The testosterone in the room rose to dangerous levels. It was so high there was a good chance she

143

might pass out from it.

"Mal is on leave."

"And just happened to stop by the club?"

The suspicion in Rome's voice had her face turning red. She leaned closer and whispered, "Behave."

He squeezed her.

"Yeah, I did. I wanted to say hi to Micah. Plus I have a membership, via my family connection."

"Have you been in Atlanta recently?"

Mal's easygoing smile dissolved, and Maria knew there would be a fight unless she stepped in.

"No, Mal was on a mission overseas. All hush-hush. So he's not a suspect."

"Did you check it out?"

The growl that rumbled from Mal's chest meant that someone was going to end up with a broken nose.

"Romeo Carino, if you don't behave, I'll make you regret it."

For a second there was a stunned silence in the kitchen.

"Romeo?" Mal asked, then he chuckled. It turned into a belly laugh.

"And you're not much better, Malachai Fredrick Dupree. You behave, or I'll tell people you get seasick."

She was satisfied to see his smile dissolve.

He gave her a dark frown. "You promised not to tell anyone."

"Yeah, well, you're both being immature. Stop it."

She crossed her arms and gave them both her meanest stare. Mal chuckled, and Rome ignored her.

"Now that you're here, I'll go. And don't worry, I'll keep your cover. Don't have much time here anyway. Just three days before I have to be back."

"I'll walk you out."

She could tell from Rome's expression that he wanted to tell her not to, but she gave him a look that let him know he would regret it.

"Thanks for seeing Maria home."

She rolled her eyes. "Yeah, the trained FBI agent needed to be seen home."

He said nothing else as she walked Mal back out to his rental.

"So you're not just on the job."

The statement was said in a way that had her temper rising. "What's that supposed to mean?"

His mouth kicked up on one corner. "Nothing."

"You know a lot of people get involved while undercover. We are both free agents in that realm, so I don't see a problem. Besides, we have to keep up the appearance that we're involved."

Malachai said nothing as he studied her. She wasn't much different. She tended to study people, watch their reactions to what was being said, to get a feel of what people were thinking. Her father had taught her how to do it years ago, and she knew Mal had training in it.

"Stop. You're not on some fucking mission."

He snorted. "Yeah? Well, I must have upset you if you're cussing. The only time you cuss is when you drink and when you're losing at chess."

She growled.

"Oh, and now you sound like your boyfriend in there."

"He's not my boyfriend."

That was a silly term, and one she wasn't ready for. Truthfully, she'd never really used that term before, so it sounded odd to her.

"Why not? He was sure acting like it in there. And although I can't see out of the back of my head, I can feel him watching us."

"He is not."

Mal nodded. "Probably out that front bay window, although it could be from the bathroom."

She looked over Mal's shoulder and saw Rome. Mortification had her face burning red. Mal just laughed in her face. "It's about time."

"What?"

"That you let a man take care of you."

She sighed and rubbed her temples. "I don't need a man to take care of me."

"No. But it's nice to have someone there you can depend on."

"Yeah, yeah, it's kind of nice. Annoying, and I am going to read him the riot act when I get in there, but definitely nice."

"I guess I should have seen it before."

She studied him for a second. "You didn't want the role."

"No, babe, the two of us were meant for other things. We both knew that from the beginning."

She nodded. Out of all her ex-lovers, Mal was the only one who understood. The only one who knew exactly what made her tick. Until Rome.

"Have you told him about the writing?"

She shook her head. "I've barely known him five days."

"Five days and you slept with him already?"

She could feel her face turning red again.

"Lord, you are hooked. I guess I can see you when I come to visit Chris, Cynthia, and Jocelyn."

She shook her head. "I still can't believe I didn't make the connection."

"We didn't talk much then, if I remember. Other than your writing and the job."

"And your job." She studied him for a moment. The summer they had met she had been green, so green she didn't even know how to hide the fact that she found him attractive. With his mocha-colored skin, hazel eyes, and that winning smile—not to mention the body of a warrior—she had been surprised when he'd been interested in her. But soon, even with a little mutual attraction, their friendship became more important than the sex. And she knew she couldn't deal with loving a man who was usually halfway around the world.

146

"How long you have?"

"Just a couple of days. I have a gut feeling we're going back out and soon, so I'm heading back to San Diego."

She frowned. Mal's gut was always right. And she hated that, hated that her friend was going to be in danger. Rationally, she knew it was stupid because that is what she trained for, as did Malachai. It was in his blood to serve and protect.

"Okay, well give me a call if you have a moment free."

He looked back over his shoulder. "You sure I should do that?"

She rolled her eyes and leaned forward to give him a kiss on the cheek. The front door opened and that had Mal chuckling again.

"Talk to you later, Maria."

She watched him drive away. Just a few moments later, she felt the brush of Rome's fingers on her bare shoulder.

"You were acting like an ass."

He slipped his hand down to her waist and pulled her closer. She felt the brush of his mouth against her temple, and she sighed.

"I know I was. I promise to be good from now on."

"Really," she said, looking at him from the corner of her eye. "And I was planning on having fun tonight."

He gave her rear a pat. "Now that I can promise."

She heard the deepening of his voice, felt the stirring within her. "Don't you want to talk about the case tonight?"

He held the door open for her. "No, Maria, I think we need to have a little chat about discipline."

Chapter Thirteen

Rome held the silky red blindfold in his hand as looked down at Maria and smiled. He had been thinking of this moment since their first night together.

She was tied up to his bed, her hands cuffed to his headboard. Her legs were stretched, cuffed to a strap that was attached to the bed. She was trying her best not to let him know how much this act unnerved her. For him, it was easy to see. Oh, she was aroused, there was no doubting that. Her breathing was hitched and there was a flush to her cheeks that had more to do with being turned on than frightened. The scent of her musky arousal filled the room.

The fear was there, though. She wasn't afraid of him, not really. His training had taught him how to discern the difference. She was frightened of the feelings rolling through her now. It was something to play at being tied up, of choosing to be someone's sub. In the act of tying her to the bed, he had taken a lot of the choice away from her. She had her own safe word, and she could have said no at any point, still could, and he would honor it. He might die from lack of blood to the brain, but he would definitely honor it.

Her gaze rested on the blindfold in his hands. He knew this was one big step for her, for them. He kept telling himself that this was just for a short time, but somewhere deep inside him he knew it was something else, something bigger.

He leaned over the bed and tied the blindfold on her. She didn't pull away or show any worries about it, but he knew she had them. For someone so much in control of everything, this was the ultimate submission. He usually didn't push his subs so far so fast, but after tonight, he felt he needed to show some kind of power, to let her know who was in control. And dammit, he had wanted to claim her.

"You have your safe word."

She nodded but said nothing. He skimmed his hand down her chest, teasing her nipples. They were tight, easily showing him how aroused she was. As he slipped his hand down her body—enjoying the way her stomach muscles quivered in reaction—he leaned forward and took a nipple into his mouth. She was so sweet, so what he needed. Women were a delight, but something about the taste of her skin, the scent of her arousal, spoke to Rome.

When he slipped his hand over her pussy, he tried to calm his own heart. It never failed to amaze him how turned on she got with just a little play. And tonight he was going to test the limits. He needed to make her understand that even for this little bit, she was his.

He dipped his fingers into her sex and sighed against her breast. So hot, so wet. He knew just how she tasted. He wanted to do nothing more than forget all of this, all the toys he had assembled, and just fuck her until they both forgot their names.

He moved away from her, needing some space. He would never accomplish the pleasures he wanted to tonight if he didn't gain some control over his own needs.

With considerable effort, he walked to the dresser and opened the drawer. He'd spent more money on toys in the last few days than he had in the last year. There was something so thrilling about showing Maria the pleasure she could gain from submission. Hell, if he wasn't careful, he would go bankrupt trying to tie her to him.

He shook that thought away. He couldn't think about tomorrow with her. Living in the moment is what would work.

Forcing his attention back to the present, he approached the bed. She wanted to squirm. Rome could read it in her expression. It was taking all her control not to do it. To reward her, he skimmed a hand up the inside of her leg. He liked that while she was muscled and in shape, there was a softness to her. He caressed her bare mound and felt his need for her rise. She was wet for him. All he had done was spank her and then tie her up. Just those two things had her close to coming.

He ran his hand across her mound, teasing her clit. "Remember, you are not to come without permission." He pinched the tiny bundle of nerves and couldn't fight a smile when she sucked in a quick breath.

Wanting to be comfortable, he slipped onto the bed next to her and picked up the vibrator. He'd bought it just for her earlier today. He wanted more, wanted to do more, but he knew that their time was limited. There was only so much he could take before he lost control. If he thought about it, he might worry. Since he'd come into the life, he'd never really had an issue. Until Maria.

He slipped the toy over her clit. She hummed. Now she did wiggle against it and let out a frustrated growl when she couldn't move. Without saying anything, he moved between her legs and settled down. He skimmed the vibrator over her dripping slit, then into her. As she moaned, he bent his head and took her clit into his mouth. He knew the dual feelings would push her right to the edge. As he felt her orgasm approaching, he moved away and turned the toy down. Over and over, he pushed her to the edge but didn't let her fall. He knew when he'd pushed her too much. "Come for me, baby."

She sighed in relief and as he pulled her clit into his mouth, she came, her body bowing as much as she could being tied the way she was. His hands were shaking when he set aside the toy and grabbed a condom. He had it on in record time, untied her feet and rose to his knees, wrapping her legs around his waist.

He entered her in one hard thrust and then started to build her back up. He wanted to feel her come again, feel all those muscles tighten around his cock.

Soon she was moaning his name again. He pulled the blindfold off and kissed her. She opened her eyes just as her second orgasm shuddered through her body. Her eyes went blind with pleasure. It was too much for him. He thrust into her twice more then came, losing himself with her in their pleasure.

. . . . .

"Hey, Rome, you have company."

Rome looked up from his desk, expecting Maria. Instead he found Malachai Dupree striding his way down the aisle. Shit, he wasn't in the mood, but from the look on the Seal's face, he wasn't going to turn around and walk away.

"Do you have a few seconds?"

"No, hello, nice to see you, Carino?"

The stoic look Dupree gave him told Rome he wasn't in the mood. There was just no way he was going to get out of this, so Rome nodded and led Dupree to a conference room.

Once they were in there, Dupree studied the room.

"No recorders or cameras?"

Rome shook his head.

"Maria told me what's going on. The whole plan."

Shit.

"Don't worry. I won't blow your cover. Hell, I hope you catch the bastard, so she can get people off her back."

"People off her back?"

"Yeah, you know being Big John Callahan's daughter has some good things and some bad things attached to it. One of the bad things being that she has to deal with people thinking she got there because of him."

"I can understand that."

"I figured that's why you lit out of Seattle. Hard to come from a family of cops and be a cop in the same city. I see it with guys who follow fathers into the military. Not always that easy to live up to. But, I digress. I said I was here to talk about Maria."

Rome crossed his arms over his chest. He didn't like the proprietary tone Dupree used when he said Maria's name. "Go on."

"I just want you to know that she might seem like she's alone in the world, but she's not."

Rome said nothing, and he could tell that irritated the Seal. More than irritated him.

"You might think you're just having a good time, but Maria is a good girl. She doesn't need some jackass messing with her head."

Aggravation marched down his spine as he tried to hold onto his temper. "Is that what you think I'm doing? That people who live the life like me are just messing with each other's head."

"No. But she doesn't need another one like you."

That gave Rome pause. "Another jackass? I thought she'd never submitted before." He was sure of it. Besides the fact that she told him, her reactions had been too raw, too real for them to have been staged. He was sure he had been her first Dom.

And her last.

Rome pushed that thought aside. "Explain yourself."

"She'll kick my ass, but she was involved with a few guys at the bureau. All of them thought she could help their careers. As soon as they figured out she couldn't, she was dumped."

"I have nothing to gain from this."

Dupree snorted. "Other than making yourself a big name

by catching a serial killer. Putting her out there to be bait."

"Hey, that was her crazy idea. And basically she told me if I didn't help, she would do it anyway without me. She didn't need my help, or so she said."

"That's what she said."

"Then why are you yelling at me?"

"I thought maybe it had been your idea to begin with."

Rome shook his head. "No. All hers. Sits there as pretty as she can be and tells me she's going to be bait for a serial killer who likes to kill women who look like her."

Mal sighed, a resigned look flashing in his face. "Damn, always fighting that old man. I thought after he died, she'd let it go."

"Oh, yeah, and I have to deal with her acting like I'm being a macho asshole because I want her to be protected as she dangles herself in front of the killer like some big, juicy piece of steak. It's enough to drive a saint to sin."

"You don't say," Mal said, rocking back on his heels.

"And she really drives me insane. She's so damned smart that she thinks she can't mess anything up, but in this game, one little slip up and she could be dead. I couldn't deal with that."

Mal said nothing for a moment then he grinned. "Shit, you're in love with her."

"What?"

"You are knee deep and drunk in love with the woman."

"No." He couldn't be. He was infatuated, like Amy said, that was all. She was so different than any of the other women he'd dated, and he really had never initiated a sub before her. It was that connection. That was all.

"Damn, this is good. You can take care of her, get her away from DC."

He was still trying to figure out if Mal was right about his feelings when what he said penetrated his brain. "Get her away from DC? What the hell are you talking about?"

"I guess you haven't had much time to chat, with chasing

153

the serial killer, huh?"

Rome shook his head.

"She's not built for the FBI."

Anger had him striding toward the Seal, ignoring the fact that there was a good chance Dupree would knock him senseless with little effort. "What the hell do you mean? She's an excellent agent. Her mind is amazing."

"Yes, but that's part of her personality. She is good at being things. Her father taught her that, may he rot in hell."

Some of his anger subsided. "I take it you didn't like him."

"I never met him, but there is something wrong with a man who teaches his fourteen-year-old daughter to shoot because there is a good chance someone will kill her."

"He told her that?"

Mal nodded. "That's just the surface. How can any teenager have a normal life going to crime scenes? Her best friends were the other agents. She became an agent because she couldn't see being anything else."

"She's damned good, probably will move up the ladder."

"And die an early death of stress. She's good at it, but she's much better at other things. Have you looked at her laptop yet?"

"Looked at it?"

Dupree smiled. "Take a minute or two, get a peek. I think you might be surprised by what you find."

"I know about the writing."

"Really? Be sure to read some of it. She's really good."

Dupree turned to leave, and Rome stopped him.

"That's it?"

"I had to make sure you weren't going to use her. I'm not going to be around for a good long while."

"Mission?"

"Just a feeling I have. Make sure you take care of her, or I will come back here and kick your ass."

With that, he slipped out of the conference room and left

Rome alone. Damn, he didn't really want to like the man, but he did. And he had to respect him. Rome knew what BUDS training was, knew what a hardass you had to be to make it through. But it still didn't mean he could take the fact that one of her ex-lovers just seemed to pop up on the island. He would definitely check out just where and when Dupree had been deployed in the last year.

That would give him something to do other than dealing with his feelings for a woman who turned out to be more complex than the serial killer they were chasing.

Chapter Fourteen

Sitting on Rome's back lanai, Maria rubbed her temples and tried to concentrate. She couldn't seem to keep anything straight. Between the lack of sleep, her involvement with Rome, and now Mal showing up, she was having a hard time doing anything but freaking out.

An agent runs a good, tight ship. Life doesn't get in the way.

Oh, put a sock in it, she thought, then instantly felt guilty. Her father had been a bad parent, especially after her mother had been killed. But in his own way, he'd been trying to teach her what he knew. The fear that some other killer would come out of the woodwork and kill her bothered him until the day he died. It had been one of the last things they had talked about. No long discussions of their lives together. No, her father had been worried that someone would kill her.

She pushed that aside and tried to work on the scene she had thought would be easy. But nothing came. With a sigh, she looked over Rome's backyard and contemplated the man himself. He'd been amazing the night before. Hell, what night wasn't he wonderful? The man knew her every emotion, everything she needed. Unfortunately, she knew nothing he needed. She wasn't even sure he needed her or if she was just a fill-in for the moment.

Dammit. She couldn't think about that. She only had a

brief amount of time to catch this bastard and then go back to
DC and prove everyone wrong. She was ready to do it, ready
to take that next step. But the moment she thought it, the
sense of accomplishment she once felt didn't seem as strong.
Maybe it was going back to DC that was bothering her. Who
could blame her. It was February. The coldest month of the
year there, usually, with its slush and snow and cold, blow-
right-through-you winds. She liked the snow, but when you
had to trudge out into it for work, it wasn't any fun. But here
she sat outside, shorts on, enjoying the cool trades as they
shifted through her hair and over her skin. It was a little hot
for her today, but every now and then a breeze would filter   ·
across the lanai, and she was content.

Her phone rang, and she frowned at the number. It was a
Hawaii area code, but not a number she knew.

"Hello?"

"Hello, pretty lady."

She recognized the accent immediately. Elias St John.

"How did you get my number, Mr. St John?"

"I have a way with people."

She said nothing. This wasn't good. The man found her
cell number, and it wasn't easy to do. She never gave it out
except for work. He must have connections, and she was
pretty sure they weren't the good kind.

"So you won't tell me the source?"

"Nope, sworn to secrecy."

She sighed, knowing there was no way she would find
anything out from him like this. "What did you want?"

"I saw you leave with another man last night."

"And?"

"I was wondering if you were a free agent yet."

"Yet? As in, there is a good chance Rome Carino will
dump me soon, so why not move on?"

He chuckled. "No. What I mean is that I thought you
would come to your senses. You're probably one of the most
spirited subs I've met in a good, long while."

She said nothing again.

"Oh, you are very good. Well, if you aren't a free agent, then I figure I will go on the hunt again. Have a good day. Remember, you have my number now if you change your mind."

She shivered as the phone clicked off.

She realized now that she needed to definitely get someone really digging things up on St John, and fast. His interest in her wasn't normal. She already had Masters running info on Ashton, although he came up clean at every turn. He was a slime, but he didn't seem to have anything in his background tying him to the killings in other cities.

. . . . .

Rome felt the weight of everything on his shoulders. This was getting too old, too fast. They couldn't figure the killer out, and now this. He could still smell the blood of the five-year-old they found today, and that of his mother who had lain dead beside him. They had been butchered by someone who was supposed to love them.

He had always felt there was good in the world, but today was one of those days that he found it hard to keep it straight. To remember that while there was evil, there was also good.

He unfolded himself from the car and shut the door. He knew Maria was there, that they would have to discuss the case, but he wasn't in the mood. He just wanted to take a shower, drink a beer, and then pass out. He trudged up the steps, his weariness increasing.

He opened the door and smelled food cooking.

"Hey, Rome. I hope you don't mind, but I thawed some chicken. I thought we could grill them."

He said nothing as he walked to the fridge to grab a beer.

"Hey, I'm checking out Elias St John. Do you know him?"

He made a noise that even to him sounded like a grunt. It was rude. He knew that. But he didn't have the energy to do any more than that.

"He called me. I'm having Masters look him up."

"What?"

"Elias St John."

"What about him?"

She frowned at him. "I talked to him last night."

"What do you mean?"

"Haven't you been listening?"

He knew there was a fight brewing, and he knew he couldn't control himself.

"Sorry, bad day. I'm going to take a shower."

He wandered off to the bathroom and knew again that he was being rude, but he couldn't seem to force himself to do anything but walk away. After setting his beer on the counter, he stripped down, dropping his clothes on the floor. He turned on the water as he took another long swig of beer. When he saw the steam gathering, he stepped into the shower, shutting the door behind him. A long soak would have been good, but he needed something pounding on his back.

The water was almost too hot, but Rome didn't care. He just let it slide over his skin as he took another long swig of beer. The shower door opened.

"I'm not good to be around right now."

She stepped in behind him and slipped her arms around his waist. She was completely naked, of course.

"I'm serious, Maria, don't mess with me now."

She rested her cheek against his back. "You can tell me about it or you don't have to. But don't shut me out."

He set his beer on the ledge and turned around to face her. Her hair was starting to curl as it did when it was really humid.

"I don't think it's a good idea to mess with me tonight."

She smiled and pressed against him. "I think your body

159

disagrees."

"Maria," he started, but he didn't finish. It was entirely her fault. She dropped to her knees in front of him. Without saying anything, she wrapped her hand around his cock and pumped him twice before taking him into her mouth. He knew he should stop her, but he didn't seem to have the ability. She continued to pump him with her hand as she worked him in and out of her mouth.

Soon, he couldn't seem to hold himself back. She stroked him with her tongue, taking him deeper into her wet, hot mouth. He felt himself grow harder and with each thrust into her mouth, he grew closer to his orgasm. Then she took him so deep, he bumped the back of her throat.

He lost himself and came, thrusting deep into her mouth. He reached down to help her up and noticed that his hands were shaking. He pulled her into his arms and leaned his forehead against hers as he tried to catch his breath.

"You didn't have to do that. Shouldn't have without permission."

She gave him a cocky smile. "I'm sure you can figure out some punishment for me."

He laughed, feeling lighter and definitely in a better mood. "After dinner."

. . . . .

Maria's phone woke her up. She opened her eyes and saw that it was only four a.m.

"Yours?" Rome asked.

"Yeah." She noticed it was Masters' number. "Please tell me this is important."

"Oh, sorry. I forgot the time difference." But he didn't sound very sorry. "I found something on St John."

She pulled herself up to a sitting position.

"What did you find?"

160

"Not much. He did some time as a jackaroo."

"A what?"

"The Aussies call their cowboys jackaroos. He worked several ranches there and then he dropped off the map for several years."

"Dropped off the map? You mean he disappeared? No one can disappear."

"He did, but I made a few calls. He was working for the Tactical Assault Group for the Aussie military."

"But there should be some kind of record, something."

"Yeah. That's what I'm trying to find out. But he has pretty much been on the Big Island for all the other assaults, so he isn't your guy."

She sighed as she massaged her temple. She could feel the telltale tension that heralded one of her bad headaches. In all the time she'd been in Hawaii, she hadn't had the familiar pain. Now it seemed to be back.

"Thanks for tracking that down. I appreciate it. He probably used his connections to get my number."

"What do you mean?" Rome asked, now completely awake.

"Who's that?" Masters asked, amusement threading his voice. Maria was pretty sure he knew who was in bed with her.

"Don't worry. I'll let you know if we have any more suspects. Are you a daddy, yet?"

"No. They plan to induce tomorrow if she doesn't go into labor by then."

"Text me and let me know how it goes."

"Will do. Behave yourself, Maria."

"I always do."

She hung up, and before she could put her phone down, she found herself on her back, Rome looming over her. She should be pissed, but of course, it aroused her. It was hard not to be turned on by Rome when he went into predatory male mode.

"Who had your number? Who called you?"

"I told you when you came home. Elias St John."

"Eli St John, that bastard. When did you meet him?"

"The night you got called away from Rough 'n Ready. He approached me after you left, but he isn't a suspect."

"Why not?"

He sounded pissed that he couldn't take St John in for questioning. If Rome wasn't a by-the-book kind of cop, he might just have done it.

"Because he was on the Big Island for all the attacks."

He growled, literally growled, as he pulled the rest of his body over hers. "So what was St John trying to do with you?"

Maria normally didn't like when men tried to exert their dominance over her. In the bedroom, while making love, that didn't bother her. But she didn't like being questioned like a suspect. But again, Rome in any kind of mood seemed to turn her on.

"Nothing much, he wanted to see if we were exclusive."

His expression darkened. "I'll kill him. Do you know where he's staying?"

He slid off the bed as he was talking and grabbed a pair of jeans. She watched with a strange mixture of frustration and amusement. It was definitely a novel experience to have a man want to do battle over her.

"No. I have no idea where he's at right now. Did you hear me say that he's not on the list of suspects?"

He gave her a dark look as he stood there. He looked so, well, lost. Maria was pretty sure he didn't realize how adorable he appeared. The idea that she could cause this was insane, but apparently she had. She rolled over to his side of the bed and rose to her knees in front of him.

"He just wanted to make sure that we were exclusive."

He grumbled.

"What was that?"

"Nothing."

162

She slipped her arms over his shoulders and inched closer to him.

"He was looking for a sub. I was alone."

"I had just left. Bastard."

She smiled, but she didn't laugh. "And I very politely said no."

Another grumble.

He wasn't looking at her, and he was still frowning. She pressed her body against his, enjoying the way his heart ticked up a beat.

"Rome."

He still didn't look at her. She kissed his jaw. "Rome."

Now he did look at her, and she smiled.

"I said no. Part of the reason was because I am an FBI agent, raised by one of the smartest FBI agents to ever wear the badge. There's a serial killer running around killing subs. I'm not an idiot."

"I didn't say you were."

"And the other reason, the bigger reason, is because I'm involved with you. Even if there was nothing to worry about, no serial killer in the picture, I would have said no. Why would I want a man like St John when I have you?"

His shoulders relaxed. "I was being an ass."

She kissed his chin. "Yeah, a little bit. Not that I didn't find it incredibly sexy."

One side of his mouth curved. "Yeah?"

"No one has ever gotten jealous over me before."

"I find that hard to believe."

"Before you, there wasn't much of a reason."

He shook his head and kissed her. "Come on, let's go back to bed."

She followed him happily.

. . . . .

Two hours later, it was Rome's phone that woke them up. "Yeah. Carino."

"Detective Carino. This is Officer Akito. We have another woman."

He stood, his mind on the work to be done. "Location."

After hanging up, he looked at Maria. "Another woman." She nodded. "I'll wait here."

Her hair was a mess, a tangle of curls dripping over her shoulders. She was naked. He sighed and gave her a quick kiss.

Traffic was light because of the early hour, so it took him no time to get to the scene. It was another alley, not too far from where he'd taken Maria to eat breakfast that first morning. Shit. There was already a crowd.

He stepped through the crowd, ignoring the questions from reporters. When he reached the alley, a young uniformed officer stepped up. "Carino."

He nodded. "What do you have?"

"Woman, twenty-eight, strangled, ME thinks she was raped."

"Do we know her identity?"

"Amy Walsh."

His heart stopped for a second then dropped to the bottom of his stomach.

"What did you say?"

He gave Rome a strange look and repeated the name. Amy.

"Are you sure?" he asked, trying to keep his emotions under control, but he could already feel his stomach roiling.

Officer nodded. "As much as we can be without a personal id."

Rome nodded and walked forward. Each step felt heavier. He had recognized the women, all of them. But Amy was different.

He walked up to Tim and his CID crew.

"Same MO?"

Tim nodded. "Looks like. This one though, he left an id."

He sighed as he looked down at Amy. He could still remember the joy on her face when she talked about her new man. She wasn't stupid, that was for sure. There was no way she would go with someone she didn't know in this part of town. Hell, he wasn't sure she would have come with someone she knew well. Even him.

"We'll get a positive ID."

"It's her," he said.

Tim looked up, studying Rome. "You know her."

"Knew. I knew her."

He pulled back in his emotions, knowing that he couldn't help her now. There was no saving Amy from whoever had done this. But he could make sure the bastard would pay.

With that last thought, he slipped on his gloves and started the job of looking for clues.

. . . . .

A long three hours later, he was summoned to the captain's office.

"Shut the door."

He did as ordered and sat down and waited for the captain to sign something.

"You knew the victim."

Rome nodded. "She hadn't been at the club for the last few months. She'd met someone. He didn't like playing at the club."

His boss didn't waste time getting down to the particulars. "Was she a member of Rough 'n Ready?"

He nodded. "As I was telling Tim, she hadn't been there recently."

The captain studied him for a moment. "You were involved with her."

He looked at the captain and nodded. "But we broke it off

a few months ago. Amicably. She'd met someone outside of the club. A Dom, but not a member of the club."

"I'm going to have to get personal here."

"Go ahead."

"For people of your persuasion, is it odd to meet someone outside of the club scene?"

He shook his head. "Not really. Easy enough to find people online. There are some dating sites that cater to just about anything."

"Shit."

"Which means, of course, that our suspect list just got longer." He thought over the murders, how they were women he had interacted with, but this one spoke of frustration. "The ME said it was more violent, he's escalating."

"And he seems to be getting closer to you."

He studied the captain's face. "No. Don't even think of taking me off the case."

"I'm not. Okay, yeah, I thought about it, but I'm not going to take you off. You're apparently working well with what's-her-name."

"Maria. Agent Callahan," he corrected.

"Keep me up to date. Find out who she was seeing, too. Make sure that it isn't another copycat."

He nodded as he rose and walked out of the office.

"Hey, Rome."

He was jolted out of his thoughts by Jack. "Hey, what are you doing here?"

"Final out processing. I had a few papers to sign."

Rome nodded, already closing down his computer so he could leave.

"How's Maria?"

"What?"

"The woman you introduced me to the other day. Maria." Jack's smile widened. "Let me guess. You've moved on all ready."

He tried to keep his temper in check. Knowing there was

a chance their killer had ties to the FBI or the police, he had to act normally. Nothing out of the ordinary or it would gain attention. He leaned back in his chair and studied his old partner. They had never really been good friends. Jack wasn't a bad cop, just a lazy one. He didn't go the extra mile to do his job, something that Rome did.

He shrugged, realizing that Jack was waiting for an answer. "Nope, still having fun with her."

"Just let me know when you're done with her. She looked like a hot piece of ass. Where is she from?'

He wanted to punch the son of a bitch in the face, but he knew that it would draw attention to them.

"Florida. Or Georgia, not really sure. With a woman like that, you don't ask too many questions."

Jack chuckled, and it grated down Rome's spine.

"I bet you don't. But then you like them all submissive, ready to do what you want."

Rome had to bite back the snarl, along with a swift right hook. Jack had always been an asshole, but his latest divorce seemed to have taken it to a whole new level.

"I heard there was another girl found last night. You might want to start thinking with your big head so that you can possibly solve the case. Having a repeat of what happened in Seattle might not be good for your career."

He offered Jack a nasty smile. From the time they were stuck together, Rome hadn't liked the bastard. He had no respect for anything, the badge especially, and Rome had been thrilled when his latest wife had decided to divorce him. Knowing the ass was leaving soon, Rome shrugged.

"Don't worry about me, Jack. Especially when you got enough on your mind as it is. I mean, how much is Tina gonna take you for?"

A flush of red darkened Jack's face, and his fingers curled into his hands. Rome knew he had punched a few buttons, mainly Tina. She was already involved with another man, happy as a clam.

But when Jack noticed the room had gone silent, he visibly pulled himself back from the rage Rome had seen in his eyes.

Rome said nothing else as he brushed past him on his way to Maria. He hadn't had much of a conversation with her earlier. Just the limited information he could tell her over the phone. He got into his car and started off to his house, thinking about Jack's comments. His old partner was an asshole that was sure, but there was a bit of the truth in what he said. Since Maria had appeared on the island, Rome had seemed to lose his focus. They were working on the case, but was he working on it enough?

He knew the answer to that, and it was a big fat no. Damned woman had him so tangled up, he didn't know how to react, and he was screwing up possibly the most important case of his career. He did have that one mark against him from Seattle. He didn't know how Jack knew about it, very few did, and he didn't truly get in trouble. Not even a reprimand. But he knew it was his fault for being so infatuated with Renee. The woman had screwed his brain while she'd been on the take. The only reason she had been with him was because of that. And working with the FBI to take her down should have satisfied him, but it hadn't.

He pushed those old memories away and concentrated on the present. He had to get his head back in the game before any other women got hurt.

Chapter Fifteen

Maria glanced around the club and tried to hold back the irritated sigh that seemed to be hovering in her constantly. It had been two days since they'd found Amy, and Rome was even more distant than ever. It wasn't anything anyone else could see, but it was something she could feel. He rubbed his fingers down her arm and leaned closer.

"You're supposed to be having fun," he said.

His warm breath feathered over her ear, and she had to fight the shiver. She would not show him anything. Two could play at his game.

She turned to him then and her heart hurt. He was so gorgeous with those dark eyes and sculpted cheekbones...but he was being an ass. Just like all men were. It had just taken her longer to find out how big of an asshole he could be.

"Am I?"

For a second he didn't say anything. "Are you what?"

"Supposed to be having fun?"

He pulled back just an inch or two, but it might as well have been a mile. Then he glanced around. "We're supposed to at least be pretending to have fun, you know, catch the killer."

She wasn't going to win the battle. Not here, not at his place, not ever. For some reason, he had decided to be distant, to barely touch her except when they were in public.

Maria didn't understand, but she rarely did. Men didn't explain, though. They just made you fall in love with them and then dumped you.

"I can pretend. But I'm not a party girl. I'm not a lot of things."

Before Rome could say anything, Micah intruded. "Hey, Rome. Maria."

Micah was studying her, as if trying to figure out what was going on. If he did, she would pay money to know what the hell was wrong with Rome. She had a feeling the club owner knew something was up between the two of them, but he was too polite to say anything.

"Rome, I was wondering if we could have a chat alone."

Rome looked at her. "Well, Maria—"

"Is a big girl, and she can take care of herself," Maria said, cutting Rome off. She needed a break from having him touch her.

"Okay, don't go anywhere." He leaned in and gave her a simple kiss. She could feel the heat of his body and could smell the wonderful unique scent of him. Then he pulled away. She watched them walk up the stairs together and sighed. The plan had been hers, all hers, and she had no one to blame but herself.

"Now, you don't sound very happy, hun."

She wanted to jump the moment she heard Eli St John's voice, but Maria forced herself not to. Slowly she turned and found him standing behind her.

"Of course, I've just been left at a table by myself."

He chuckled and sat down without invitation. She raised one eyebrow.

"If I waited for an invite, you might never ask me. This way, I can get my objective done and fast enough so I don't have to deal with your boyfriend."

She blinked. "I don't have a boyfriend."

He cocked his head to the side and studied her. "Looked like it from where I sat."

He'd been watching her. It didn't give her the same feeling as when she knew Rome was watching her. This made her feel…dirty.

"What do you want, St John?"

He laughed then, a loud one that boomed off the walls. It was so loud people at the surrounding tables heard it over the music.

"I sure do like you, Maria. Why are you wasting time with Rome Carino?"

"You think I am? Why is that?"

"Word is that he doesn't last too long with women. A few weeks here and there, maybe a month or two, then he tosses them aside."

Was that what he was doing? Probably. But she refused to let St John know. He wasn't a suspect, so she relaxed against the seat and decided to flirt. It would be good if the killer saw her being flirty with another man. It might draw more attention to her.

"And what is it you're offering?"

"Well, now, I can offer some fun on a ranch. Do you like horses?"

· · · · ·

Rome could feel his skin crawling. It felt as if there were thousands of ants climbing all over him. He rolled his shoulders and tried to pull himself back under control.

"So you have no other evidence?" Micah asked.

"No. He's getting bolder and more violent. Much more violent."

Micah nodded as Rome rose and started pacing the office. He couldn't sit still. Granted it was his fault. He hadn't touched Maria in the last two days other than their time at the club. If she knew just how each little brush of his fingers on her flesh drove him insane, she gave no indication. Worse, it

171

put him in the mood for a fight. He needed some kind of physical release.

"You need to just give in, bra."

He stopped and frowned at Micah. "What the fuck are you talking about?"

Micah grinned. "Jesus, you're as bad as Evan. Give up, you're lost to her now."

"I'm not lost at all."

"You've been up here less than five minutes, and you can't stand it."

"She's made herself bait to a killer."

"And she's in the middle of a club. He didn't abduct them from a crowded area. We would have heard of that by now."

That much was true, but he didn't care. "Still."

"There is something else bothering you. And it has a lot to do with the woman and not the case."

"They're one in the same."

"Really? So when this is done, you won't touch her again."

"I'm not touching her now."

Micah snorted. "You don't have to lie to me."

"I decided two days ago I'd lost my focus."

For a moment, his friend said nothing. "And so you decided to pull back, to not touch her."

Rome nodded once.

"Romeo, you definitely don't live up to your name."

"Fuck you."

"Well, two uses of fuck in one night? You really are frustrated." Micah shook his head. "Your focus is for shit because all you can think about is her."

That was a little too close to the truth, so he did what he could. He growled at Micah.

"Hey, I'm just observing what's going on here. You're in love with the woman, and you're screwing it up. I understand you have a job, but you need to make sure you don't lose her."

Panic clutched at his throat. He wasn't in love with her. He couldn't be. She was…not right for him. He wasn't ready to settle down. And she had a life back in DC. Not that he couldn't transfer there to be near her.

Fuck.

"Bullshit."

"So you don't mind that St John is down there making the moves on her?" Micah asked, nodding his head toward the monitors.

Rome whipped his head around and another growl rumbled in his chest. "Bastard."

He didn't say anything else. He just stomped out of the room, down the stairs, his sights set on St John and Maria. She laughed at something the Aussie jackass said and St John took it as an invitation and moved closer. Fury churned in his gut as he ignored people left and right, striding through the club. Maria was still laughing when she caught sight of him. Her eyes widened, alarm easy to see. St John apparently realized she was looking behind him, and he turned around. The smile he gave Rome made him want to punch the bastard.

"It's time to go, Maria."

From her frown he could tell that she wasn't happy with his behavior.

"I thought we'd stay a little longer. Eli was telling me about his ranch on the Big Island. Have you ever been?"

"No."

"I—"

"Now."

Her face flushed red. "Rome." The admonition in her voice made him even madder. She was embarrassed? How did she think he felt watching another man paw all over her?

"Hey, Carino, you might want to take it easy." St John rose and faced him. The look on his face told Rome he was ready to fight if needed.

"This isn't your business."

173

"It is if the lady doesn't want to go home with you."

Maria popped up out of her seat then. "I do want to go, as long as Rome quits being an ass."

The warning got a grunt from him. He was going to discuss her behavior when they got out of there.

She turned to St John. "I'll get back with you on the tour, Eli. Thanks for the info."

"Anytime, Maria."

He kissed her hand and another growl vibrated in Rome's chest. No one else heard, but he knew Maria had. She gave him a nasty look and well, hell, he gave her one right back. He was sick and tired of this shit, and he wanted out of there.

He placed his hand on the small of her back and guided her through the club. When they got outside, Maria stopped.

"What the hell was that about?"

Several people glanced in their direction as they walked down the sidewalk.

"Not here."

She looked around, turned on her heels, and strode back to his car. The problem was that with her anger, her hips swayed even more. He followed after her, but he couldn't take his gaze from her ass. She reached his car and turned to face him. When she saw where his attention was, she rolled her eyes. He opened her door, and she slipped in. He walked around the hood of the car, trying to calm himself. He had gotten his temper under control. But then she'd had to speak.

"Get one thing straight, we will have this out, at my place," she said.

He wanted to shout at her, but he looked over at the entrance of the club and saw St John standing there. Shit.

"Fine. We will have it out."

With that, he turned on the car, put it in gear and punched the gas. They were definitely going to have this out.

. . . . .

Maria's temper was frayed by the time they arrived at
Rome's house. He could have gone to her rental, but of
course, he had wanted to be on his turf. The second he put
the car in park, she practically jumped out of it and slammed
the door shut behind her.

Rome gave her a dirty look. Oh, now he wanted to pay
attention to her. He had no right to be mad. She said nothing,
silently fuming until they got inside. As she had become
accustomed to, she took off her shoes as they entered. Then,
without looking behind her, she marched down the hallway
to the kitchen. It was the furthest room from the bedroom. It
was too depressing to be there. In the last forty-eight hours,
he hadn't touched her in private. In public, oh, he was all
over that, she thought with a sneer. But in private, he acted
like she was a leper.

"I will not allow you to behave the way you did tonight."

His eyebrows rose. "I don't think I need your permission.
That's not how this goes."

Frustration pushed a growl out of her before she could
contain it. "How what goes? The investigation? Both of us
know that I'm playing nice with you, but if I wanted to, I
could make sure that I had final say on everything."

His face flushed with anger, but when he spoke, his voice
was calm. "I'm talking about this relationship."

She snorted, trying to cover the pain, and crossed her
arms over her chest. "Relationship? We have one?"

He took a step toward her, his expression forbidding. "Of
course we have one. Enough of one to keep you from trying
to replace me with St John."

Jesus, the man was an idiot. "I thought our relationship
ended two days ago."

"I never said that."

"And you haven't touched me since then." She shrugged,
feigning nonchalance. "I figured I was a free agent, and it
would help with the investigation."

The look that moved over his face had her backing up a

175

step. Her rear end hit the counter, but he didn't stop moving toward her.

"Was it all about work?" he asked, his voice so serious, so dangerous, she felt a lick of fear coil in her belly.

She shook her head.

"I didn't think so. I mean, when you were screaming out my name when you came all over my cock, you didn't seem to be trying to earn any brownie points."

She swallowed, trying to get ahold of her fear. Worse, there was a sliver of sick excitement that threaded through the alarm. Maria didn't know which should bother her worse.

"As my sub, you aren't supposed to give me your opinions."

"In the bedroom," she said, amazed she got the words out. "You don't own me, Rome."

Heat flared in his hazel eyes, and she felt it churn through her blood. She shouldn't be turned on, shouldn't have the dual feelings twisting through her. But for some reason, she did. God help her, she did.

He grabbed her by the waist and lifted her up, then dropped her on the counter. Before she could protest, he was kissing her. His tongue plunged into her mouth over and over. Even as he assaulted her mouth, he was working the hem of her dress up. She wasn't wearing anything beneath it. She was already aroused, liquid heat filling her sex, her nipples tightened almost painfully.

Rome pulled away then, unzipped his pants and cursed. He pulled his wallet out, pulled a condom out, and dropped the billfold on the floor. The need coursing through her now exploded. She needed this, needed him now. He slipped the condom on then entered her, hard, swift, and although she was prepared, she drew in a quick breath. He said nothing as he moved in and out of her. Maria wrapped her legs around him and moaned.

All of a sudden, he stopped and looked up at her. It was as if he just realized what had happened.

"Maria," he said. She hated seeing the regret in his expression, the way it darkened his eyes. She took his face in her hands and kissed him, murmuring against his lips. Then he began to move again, with just as much power, but there was a difference in the way he kissed her. She still felt wanted, felt the wave of her orgasm approaching, but there was something different in the way he touched her. Soon she was coming, her body arching into his as he followed her, her name on his lips.

Their harsh breaths were the only sound as he wrapped his arms around her as if he were afraid she would leave. He looked up at her. "I'm sorry."

She shook her head and opened her mouth.

"Not for this. For being a pain in the ass."

She nodded. "I understand."

He kissed her sweetly, his gaze still latched onto hers. Maria couldn't help the way her heart trembled before falling at his feet. How could she not fall for a man like Rome? He was difficult and moody, but he made her feel like the most beautiful woman in the world.

He pulled away from her and then lifted her into his arms. He kicked off his pants. "I think I have some apologizing to do."

She smiled at him, settling her arms over his shoulders. "I believe you do, Detective Carino."

He chuckled, and she ignored the warning in her head. She would follow her heart and live with the consequences later. He set her on the bed, stripped her out of her clothes, and then joined her. As she sighed his name, her worries dissolved, and Maria lost herself in the pleasure he gave her.

· · · · ·

Maria had just poured her first cup of Kona for the day when her cell phone went off. She sighed when she saw her

177

supervisor's number. He hadn't been happy when she reported the last killing.

"Callahan."

"We got another one."

Her heart stuttered. "Here?"

"No, apparently our boy is on the move. LAPD has reported a killing in Orange County. Same MO, though she was found in a residential area."

She saw something out of the corner of her eye and realized Rome had joined her. "Was she a member of a club?"

"We're still checking, but it looks like the same thing. You need to get your ass to LA."

"But, sir, until we know for sure, shouldn't I stay here?"

Desperation was clawing at her insides, her pulse kicking up a notch. She couldn't leave. She glanced at Rome and noticed he'd stopped working on his tie.

"No, it's a short enough flight that you can get there and go back if it isn't. Masters can't make it because his wife is in labor right now."

"Oh. Okay. I'll call about a flight, leave tomorrow."

"You leave tonight, ten o'clock. I'll email everything to you."

"Yes, sir."

He hung up before she finished her agreement. She clicked off her phone and felt Rome shift closer.

"I have to go to LA. They found a woman there, same MO. He wants me on a flight tonight."

The silence lengthened. She glanced at Rome and found him staring at her with the weirdest look on his face.

"Rome?"

He sighed. "I guess we knew you would have to go back."

She blinked back the tears. Why did it feel like this was the worst thing in the world? She had realized last night, even after they made love, that there was nothing here for her.

Rome apparently didn't want long term, and while he liked to have her in his bed, he wasn't looking for something permanent. The connection they had made the night before had made her heart tremble, her knees go weak, but she knew that in part, it was leading up to the end. They both knew this was going to happen even before it started.

"Well, I guess I should go pack."

She brushed past him, but he circled his fingers around her wrist and pulled her closer. "I gotta go into the office, but I'll meet you back here this afternoon. We can do an early dinner before you fly."

She smiled, although it felt brittle. "Okay. Sounds good."

He brushed his mouth over hers and let her go. "I've got a meeting with the captain, or I would just call in. He'll definitely want to know about this. Give me a call if anything else happens."

She nodded and watched until the front door shut. The sound of it echoed through the house, and it hurt. Dammit, it hurt so much. The tears she had kept at bay now filled her eyes, and for once in a very long time, she let them flow. A woman who was losing the best man she'd ever known had a right to cry like a baby.

· · · · ·

Rome was finishing up some work after his meeting with the captain when he felt someone standing next to his desk. He glanced up and found Jack standing there. Shit, he wasn't in the mood for another confrontation.

"Hey, Rome."

"Whatya want, Jack?"

He sighed and sunk down into the chair Rome kept for visitors. "I wanted to apologize for being a jackass the other day."

Rome glanced at him, surprised. In the year he had

worked with Jack, he never once apologized for anything. "Why?"

Jack shrugged. "I know I was out of line. The divorce has left me raw. I need to put a muzzle on it."

"Then apology accepted."

Jack smiled. "Great. I'm on my way off the island since I just got word I landed a job at LAPD, but I wanted to make sure that you weren't pissed at me. I just wanted to make sure you know I'm not after your lady friend. I was just ticked because my life is going to crap."

Knowing that the killer was gone, that the ruse was up, Rome leaned back in his chair. "Not that my life is better."

"With a woman like that Maria, can't be too bad."

"She's on her way back to the mainland. She has a job to do."

"I thought maybe you were thinking about making it permanent."

His heart jolted at the idea. Keep Maria forever? Or rather, he could go to DC. Sure, he loved Hawaii, but there was part of him that would die if he let her go. His heart already felt like it had been beaten and bruised, and she hadn't even left yet.

"Not sure I could live in DC."

Jack frowned. "She lives in DC?"

"Yeah. Truth is, she's FBI working on the The Dom case. We were working undercover together, but it didn't seem to work out."

A strange expression moved over Jack's face and then it vanished. "That sucks for you."

He nodded. "When you leaving?"

"Tonight. I have a ten o'clock flight."

"Into LA? Maria might be on your flight."

"Imagine that." He rose to stand. "I have some more papers to sign, and then I gotta check out of the hotel I stayed in last night."

Rome offered his hand. "Good luck."

180

Jack smiled and shook it. "Thanks, man."

He left then and Rome watched him. If anything, it was good to know Jack had his life somewhat back on track. He was a good detective, but the home problems had made it hard for him to concentrate on the job.

Rome sat back down and decided to blow through the paperwork he had left so he could get back to spend some time with Maria.

. . . . .

Maria shut her suitcase and sniffled. She'd had a good cry while she'd folded and packed her things, but now was the time to get that stiff upper lip her father always told her to have. She felt it tremble, and she put her fingers against it. There would be no regrets. She couldn't have them. Moving on and doing what she wanted to do was the most important thing. The one thing her time with Rome and on the case taught her was that she was a good FBI agent. She hated it, though. She dreaded the idea of going back to LA and investigating. Life is too short not to do what you want, she told herself.

Before she could start crying again, the doorbell rang. She dabbed her eyes as she walked to the door. When she looked through the peephole, she was surprised at the visitor.

She composed herself with a few breaths and opened the door.

"Hey, Maria," Jack said. "Thought I would come by and say aloha."

181

Chapter Sixteen

Rome walked through his front door and was sort of surprised at the stillness. Maria could be quiet, but she wasn't that quiet. If anything, she would still be packing. She was a woman who liked everything just so.

He walked through the house, the floors squeaking beneath his feet as a sense of wrongness surrounded him.

"Maria?"

No answer. Fuck. He walked all the way through the house and found nothing at first. Had she left not wanting to face him? But then he saw her suitcase sitting open on the bed, a few more items still waiting to be packed.

"Maria!"

He ran through the house, drawing his weapon. Her laptop was on the desk in his guestroom where she kept it. Panic and fear now twisted his gut. When he heard her phone ringing, he ran to the kitchen.

He saw the two-zero-two area code and knew it was someone she worked with.

"Hello."

There was a pause. "This is Agent Smith. I'm looking for Maria Callahan."

"This is Officer Carino, and I'm also looking for Maria."

"Oh, Carino. Is Callahan around?"

Aggravation marched down his spine. He knew he didn't

have time for this. "No. I can't find her."

Another pause. "Is that normal?"

"No. Not normal at all."

"I'm trying to get ahold of her to tell her that we're cancelling the flight. The LA killing was an ex."

"Just like the one in Dallas and Sara."

"What?"

He didn't realize he had spoken out loud until the agent spoke. "We had a woman here, ex killed her. At first they thought it might be The Dom, but it didn't fit."

"What I want to know is why you have her phone and where the hell is she?"

"I'll ask her that as soon as I find her."

He hung up without waiting for an answer. He was heading toward the door when the bell rang. When he opened it, he found Tina, Jack's wife. Her face was beat all to hell, her lip split, her left eye black, and her nose had definitely been broken.

"Tina, hun, what happened to you?" he asked.

"I'm sorry to bother you Rome, but I had nowhere else to go. It's Jack, he went crazy today."

She stepped into the house. When she stood next to him, he was reminded of her petite frame. She didn't even reach his shoulder.

"No, don't worry." Even as he said it, he had half his mind on Maria and where she might be.

"Like I said, I didn't know where to go. I was furious when I found the stuff, and when I confronted Jack, he freaked. I have never seen him like that."

He showed her over to his couch, trying his best to keep his patience in check. The poor woman had been worked over.

Once she was settled, he asked, "Now, why don't you tell me what you're talking about?"

She drew in a deep breath. Rome watched as she physically pulled herself together. "I was going through his stuff, getting it ready for him to pack up this morning. I found this plastic bag, looked like one of those evidence bags you all use."

"What was in the bag?"

"Panties."

"Panties?" The worry he had earlier was now blossoming into full-blown panic.

"Yeah, there were lots of them. At first I didn't think anything of it. I mean, it would have been wrong if he had brought them home and they were evidence. He could get in trouble. I know he isn't a great cop. He lied. He said that you were never doing your job. That he had to pull up the slack."

That was interesting since Rome had been the one who had always done the heavy lifting. Jack was always too busy to do the paperwork.

"So you asked him about the panties?"

She nodded and squeezed her eyes. A fresh wave of tears came pouring out.

"He just exploded. I didn't expect it."

"Jack hadn't hit you before?"

She drew in another breath. "No, not really. He wanted to…he wanted to do some stuff while we were having sex that I wasn't comfortable with, but that was it."

Rome studied her bent head. "What kind of stuff?"

She glanced up then looked back down. "He wanted to tie me up. That didn't bother me that much. God, I can't believe I have to talk about this with you."

"I didn't think he was into BDSM."

"That wouldn't have been bad, really, but he tried to tie a scarf around my neck."

Rome's heart almost stopped beating. Son of a bitch.

"And with the panties, the thing that upset me was the scarf that was there. It was the one he'd used on me. I thought maybe he had been cheating on me while we were still together, and when I accused him of it, that was when he went crazy."

"Do you know where he is?"

She shook her head. "He left, and I took myself to the hospital. They wanted to call the cops, but I wanted to come to you. He took the bag with him, Rome."

"You did the right thing. Is your new boyfriend here?"

She shook her head. "And he's going to be so mad at me for doing this when he wasn't home, but Jack told me he was leaving tonight, and I wanted to get rid of his things. Mike's on the Big Island for business."

"Okay. I want you to come with me, we're going to go to the department, and you will file a report against him."

She nodded, and he was thankful for that. If he'd had to fight her on it, he might have lost it then and there. One thing was for certain, he didn't care what he had to do, he was going to find Maria, and if Jack was still alive, he was going to kill the bastard with his bare hands.

. . . . .

Maria came awake abruptly, the sharp smell of ammonia assaulting her.

"That's right, Maria, Ms. FBI Agent. Wake up and show me those baby blues."

She did and realized that Jack was standing close to her. So close that she could smell the musky scent of his sweat. Jack leaned down closer, bending at the waist. She tried to jerk away, but realized she couldn't get any further. She tried to move her hands, but they were bound behind her.

"Tsk, tsk." He shook his head. "Someone would think that you didn't like me."

He straightened. "I couldn't believe it when Carino told me you were an FBI agent. Who would have thought such a luscious piece of ass like you worked for the F…B…I?"

He trailed a finger down her cheek. Inwardly she cringed, but she didn't show it to him. He would get off on her fear.

"So Rome told you about me?"

Jack pulled away. "Yes. Well, not on purpose. See, he thought you were leaving, was not going to see you again, and his heart was breaking. Poor, poor Rome. He is never lucky in love. The women he's had never seem to last."

"Let me guess. You're Amy's fiancé. The one nobody could find."

He offered her a smile that sent a fresh wave of icy fear down her spine. "Guilty. She was really easy to get to. She was feeling lonesome after my old partner dumped her. Rome apparently has an issue with commitment, but you know all about that."

"Like it matters to me?"

It did, but she would be damned if she would let the bastard know.

"No? Well, women like you are married to your job." He sniffed. "Very unfeminine."

She said nothing but kept watching. He was pouring chloroform on a cloth. The sickly sweet smell was easy to detect.

"So you came behind Rome, went after his leftovers."

"I know what you're trying to do, agent. I've had the training."

But there was a tremor in his hand. She had gotten to him.

"Oh, okay. I mean, I guess you don't mind being the 'sloppy seconds' guy."

His smile tightened as he walked back to her, but he said nothing.

"I am sure it doesn't mean you can't get your own woman."

"I've had my own woman."

"Rome split with them, then you came in behind. They're vulnerable, needy, and you can satisfy a woman like that."

"Shut the fuck up." His face was turning red.

"They never seem to stick around with you, though. Is

186

that the problem you had with Amy? Or was it that she started to compare you to Rome? Did they all do that, so you had to go after them? Kill them?"

"You fucking bitch," he screeched. He gave her the back of his hand with so much force the chair tipped over onto the ground. Her head slapped against the cement floor, and she saw stars.

Then she felt his hand slip behind the back of her head, and he pressed the cloth against her mouth and nose. She struggled for a moment and then everything faded to black.

. . . . .

Rome's nerves were riding a fine line between panic and rage. Fucking hell, he should have seen it. He had dropped off Tina at the department and told them to put a trace on Jack's phone. He wasn't even out of the parking lot when his phone went off.

"Carino," the captain said. "We got a GPS track on his phone. He has her on Sand Island. Warehouse."

The idea had his gut churning. Jack must have had her for at least four hours, and the thought of what he could have done to Maria during that time… He shook his head. He would not think about it.

"The address?"

The captain rattled off an address. "I'm sending backup. The FBI had to be notified since she's an agent."

"Tell them to approach without sirens."

He hung up without getting the agreement. Right now the only thing that matter was getting to Maria.

Several long moments later, Rome pulled up to the building. There wasn't a way to really sneak into some place like this.

He found a side door unlocked. It was easy, too easy. His suspicions were confirmed when he stepped inside.

"Nice of you to join us, Rome," Jack said.

He followed the sound of his old partner's voice and found him in the storage area. He looked horrible, as if he hadn't slept in days, and Rome didn't miss the gun in Jack's hand. There was a battered table on one side and to the left of that sat Maria. His head about fell to his feet when he saw her. She had a bloody nose, a split lip, and she was tied to a chair. She looked like she was unconscious.

"It took you long enough."

He glanced at the man he used to trust with his life. Rome knew then he should have seen the signs. They had been all over the place.

"Well, I had a chat with Tina. She had a lot to say about your relationship."

He laughed. The sound of it sent a sick ball of dread to his stomach. He inched closer and saw that Maria was still breathing. He drew in a deep breath and decided he needed to get her out of there, away from the maniac. Then he could deal with the bastard.

"She's okay. You know I wouldn't hurt her until you showed up. Well, not much. She did struggle a bit, so I had to use chloroform on her twice, but she should be okay."

"Tina's giving a statement at the station. Oh, and she called that Mike guy. Someone told me he used to fight in the ring...he apparently has plans to tear you apart."

Jack's eyelid twitched. "What do I care?"

"You should. You'll lose that job you have in LA."

Jack shrugged like he didn't care, but Rome knew that he did. It was all coming apart now, which made Jack even more dangerous. He had nothing to lose.

"I'll figure something out. I always do. As my mom always said, I'm a smart boy."

Rome cocked his head to one side. "Really? I would have thought she said you were a loser."

Jack's finger twitched on the trigger. "You're wrong."

"Isn't that why you attack women? Because you could

never deal with mommy being such a total bitch?"

"Shut the fuck up."

"Or, hey, maybe it was the other way. Did she smother you?"

Jack said nothing, his face turning redder by the minute.

"Did she treat you like you were a man...like a real man? That's it, isn't it? What did Mommy do to you? Did she make you sleep with her when it was way past time to do that?"

"You don't know what the fuck you're talking about. Romeo Carino, who sleeps with his partners, who trusts the wrong partners. How the fuck are you going to get yourself out of this one? Huh? How will you make sure to convince the HPD that you aren't a total fuckup. I'm a killer, your last partner in Seattle was dealing arms, and this one," he said, waving the gun in Maria's direction, "is going to be killed."

"Oh, I don't think it will be a problem. I didn't hire you, someone else did. That person will probably get fired because you should never have passed the psych evaluation. Hell, I'd be amazed you would be able to clean toilets with any evaluation."

"Shut up," he said, swinging the gun back in Rome's direction. "You don't know what you're talking about. I know how to ace those things. Easy."

"If you didn't, I know what they would say. Aggression issues toward women. Uncontrollable temper, psychotic. All because his mommy liked to touch him."

"I said to shut the fuck up."

Rome noticed that Maria moved her foot.

"Why don't you tell me whose fault this is?"

"What?" Jack asked, his attention temporarily snagged on the question.

"If you aren't at fault, which I'm sure you're not, who did it? Who causes you to do the things you do?"

"You have no idea what it's like dealing with this. My father—," he drew in a deep, shuttering breath. "My father

189

was a bastard."

Sweat was gathering on Jack's lip, and his eyes were starting to glaze a bit. Rome knew the signs of someone going into a complete psychotic episode, and he couldn't take the chance. When Jack looked away for a moment, Rome looked at Maria. She was awake, and so he nudged his head in Jack's direction. She gave him a slight nod but allowed her head to drop forward again.

"So, why don't you tell me all about that bastard?"

"Man didn't know how to treat his family."

"But, I thought it was just you and your mother."

Jack shuddered. "No. He didn't live with us. We were Daddy's other family."

"Ah, so you're a bastard, too."

He walked back toward Rome, his gun leveled at Rome's chest. He stood close to Maria.

"Shut up. Just shut up."

"Your father didn't want you, and when he was sick of you and your mother, he left. He left you alone with a sick woman. A woman who didn't know any boundaries. And she turned you into some kind of freak. A freak who doesn't know how to be a real man."

"I said, shut up—"

His voice ended on a scream, and Maria toppled herself and the chair against Jack. Rome rushed forward, but Jack's gun discharged. He felt the sting of the bullet in his shoulder, the burning, but he ignored it. He was on Jack, taking his gun away as they fought back and forth. He gained the upper hand and straddled the bastard's chest. He hit him several times and then wrapped his fingers around his neck.

"Rome, stop. Rome."

Maria was standing next to him, grabbing on his arm. They were surrounded by FBI agents, and it took him a moment to realize they had come in the moment the gun went off. He released Jack's neck and rose. He needed to touch her, to make sure she was okay. He pulled her into his arms.

"Oh, baby, I'm so sorry."

She shuddered against him. "It's not your fault."

He blinked as his vision started to blur. "I should have known. Should have figured it out."

"Rome?"

The room was spinning, and Maria sounded like she was far away. Very far away. But she was there in his arms.

"Rome, honey, you need to sit down."

"No. I'm fine. Don't worry about me."

"Rome!"

The spinning increased, and his vision dimmed to black.

Chapter Seventeen

Maria watched him sleep. It had been a long night. The shot hadn't been life-threatening, but Rome had lost a lot of blood. She closed her eyes and said a little prayer. She didn't know how many times she had done that in the last few hours.

The door opened quietly, and Micah stuck his head in. "Hey."

She smiled then winced at the pain radiating from her lip. "Damn, that hurt."

Micah stepped inside, and he was followed by Evan. "How's he doing?"

"Okay. Nothing big, although because of the fight, he lost a little bit of blood. That's why he fainted."

"I did not faint."

She looked at Rome, surprised he was awake. The nurse had said he would be out a few more hours.

"What do you call it?"

"Women faint. Men pass out."

She rolled her eyes then looked at his friends. They were both grinning at her. "As you can see, he's fine."

Her voice caught at the end. Evan tossed her a sympathetic look. "You have to be exhausted. First you had to save his ass and then you had to sit here all night."

"Hey."

192

Both his friends ignored him. "Why don't you call your boss? There are also a couple of FBI agents hanging out in the hallway wanting to talk to you again."

She rolled her eyes as she rose. "I already talked to them."

"You don't have to talk to them now. You can just say the hell with them and stay here," Rome said, frowning. The tone in his voice made him sound like a petulant child, but she knew part of it was being in the hospital. Neither of them were very good at being patients, she was sure.

She kissed his forehead. "I have to call my supervisor anyway. I'll be right back. Don't let him get agitated."

She tried to walk by Evan, but he drew her into his arms and gave her a hug and a kiss on the cheek. "Thank you."

Then he handed her over to Micah, and he did the same. "We owe you one, Agent Callahan."

Tears burned the back of her eyes, but she blinked them away. She looked over at Rome who was watching them with a frown.

"I'll be back in a few minutes."

She slipped out of the room, relieved to be out of there. Rome had been giving her such a strange look. Almost angry. Like it had been her fault. Leaning against the wall, she shut her eyes and tried to keep from allowing the fear that had swamped her the night before to take over. She would not let it win.

"Agent Callahan?"

She opened her eyes and found the agent she'd talked to the night before. "Agent Brewer."

The man smiled at her as if her remembering his name was a gift. "If you have a chance, I'd like to talk to you. Agent Smith is on his way here."

Her eyes widened at the news. "He is?"

"Yes. He has been calling every thirty minutes to check on you."

She smiled. "He's a family friend."

"This family friend wants to know just what the hell you were thinking."

She looked down the hall at her supervisor. He looked tired. She had always thought of him as an honorary uncle. He and her father had started at the Academy together, came up in the ranks together, and it was Smith who had been beside the bed with her when her father died. Everything she had been holding back came bubbling to the surface. The fear for Rome, for herself, the stress she'd been working under the last two weeks...

She let the tears fall as she walked down the hall to him. When she reached him, he opened his arms, and she allowed him to pull her close. And then she wept.

. . . . .

"You fainted," Evan said, chuckling. "Wuss."

"I didn't faint."

"Maria said you did," Micah said as he settled in the chair beside the bed. The one Maria had been sitting in. All night, he had known she was there. He had been drugged to the gills, but he had felt her presence, and it was the only thing that would have kept him in that hospital room.

"She's wrong."

"I have a feeling she's hardly ever wrong," Micah remarked. There was a hint of humor in his friend's voice, but Rome ignored it.

"She thinks she knows what she's doing. Damned if she just thinks she can do what she wants."

Evan and Micah shared a look.

"And another thing, how does she get off acting like she saved me? I'm the one who got her out of the situation."

"Jack was your partner," Micah said quietly.

The guilt crashed down on him. "Yeah, I know. It's something I should have seen."

"Shit, son, no one could have seen it. He hid it well. His name isn't even Jack Daniels."

That caught his attention.

"What do you know?"

"Just what that Agent Brewer told us. They started looking into his background. Jack Daniels died twenty-two years ago. He stole the kid's identity, built a life for himself. I have a feeling the FBI will be uncovering information about the bastard for years."

"Maria blames herself, Rome," Micah said.

"He was my partner. I should have known he was killing women. Hell, I didn't even make the connection with all his trips back to the mainland."

"From what I heard, they're going to have a special commission, and your girlfriend is going to be under the microscope," Evan said.

"What the hell are you talking about? They're blaming her for their idiocy? Feels like she's going to be the scapegoat. They couldn't find the man, and she has to come up with some kind of asinine idea of using herself as bait, and this is the way they treat her?"

"Yeah, well, she's a trained FBI agent." Micah's tone was oddly neutral.

"So." It sounded very immature, but he didn't care. The fear he'd had when he knew that Jack had her, what he could have done to her, came rushing back. "If she thinks that she's going to be doing shit like that after we get married, she has another think coming."

"You're getting married? You proposed?" Evan asked.

"No, but we will."

"You will?" Micah asked. "Is she coming to live here?"

Rome hadn't gotten that far. Hell, he'd just come up with the idea. He couldn't let her go, couldn't watch her leave. It would tear him apart. He loved her, loved her like crazy, and there was just no way he could let her go.

"I'll probably have to move to DC."

195

"You hate DC," Evan said. "You called it a cesspool."

"That was the Pentagon. And it doesn't matter. As an FBI agent, she would have to be there. They can't move around as easily."

"You might want to ask her about that," Micah said.

Rome shook his head. He couldn't do that. Truth was, he wasn't sure she would say yes to moving to Hawaii. He was worried if he asked her to choose between her career and him, he would lose out. That he couldn't have.

"No. She's probably going to easily end up a hero in this. She put her life on the line, picked up that it was someone in law enforcement, and with me, she defeated the bastard. So her career should take off. I can easily get a job there."

Even if it would kill him. Hawaii was his home, his love, but he couldn't be here without her. She was more important to him than anything in the world.

"No, I'll move to DC."

. . . . .

"We have no idea who he is."

She stared at her supervisor. "What do you mean?"

"We have taken his prints, his DNA, nothing. But the bastard has no record. Nothing to link him to any other identity."

She sipped the water he had given her and looked out the window. The sun was just peeking over the mountains, and she sighed.

"So he stole an identity?"

He nodded. "Kid who died of leukemia. He invented a whole life."

"Not good that we didn't pick up on that."

"Us?" Her supervisor crossed his arms over his chest. "No. Three police departments hired him. Hell, he turned down a detective position with Phoenix to come here."

"Do you know anything else?"

He shook his head. "He wasn't really fixated on Rome until he came here. It was hard to work with a man who had so much respect. Jack had little from what I have been told. The other officers didn't like working with him."

She nodded.

"There's going to be an investigation at some point, but the fact that you picked up that he was in law enforcement will definitely get you some leverage. I have a feeling you'll end up with a promotion out of this."

"What?"

"Oh, don't look so stunned. You caught a serial killer that has been haunting us for two years. You got caught by him, but by doing that, I'm sure you'll end up with a promotion. Might mean you have to move. I do know there will be an opening in the Phoenix field office."

She waited for the joy that should bring, but there was nothing there. Nothing that made her feel good about getting a promotion. It should have made her ecstatic, but it didn't. In fact, she felt somehow deflated.

"Now, agent, you'll explain just what the hell you were doing."

She shook herself out of her thoughts. "Catching a killer."

"No. Your phone was left at this Detective Carino's house. What were you doing there?"

"Are you asking me about my personal relationship with Rome?"

"Yes."

"As my supervisor or as my honorary uncle?"

"As your father's best friend. Just what the hell is it? I hear you were going to a BDSM club with him, living with him? Was that just part of the job?"

Not for her. She shook her head.

"And just what the hell is going to happen between you two?"

"Are you by chance asking me if his intentions are honorable?"

He looked uncomfortable, but he nodded. "Someone has to."

"I wasn't a virgin. I'm close to thirty."

"And you might be able to fool other people, but I know that none of your relationships were like this."

She straightened her spine. "Keeping tabs on me?"

His expression softened, and he reached across the table to pat her on the hand. "No, honey. I hear it when you say his name. You're in love with him."

The tears started to burn the back of her eyes again, but she would not cry. She would not fall apart again. "Yes."

"So, what ya going to do about it, little girl?"

"Nothing. Rome isn't into long-term relationships, and I knew that when I went into the this. Don't worry about me. I can handle it."

The look he gave her told her that he thought otherwise.

"I have to talk to you about something else," she said.

"What would that be?"

"My future at the FBI."

. . . . .

"You didn't have to drive home."

Rome was grumbling, and he knew he sounded like a little boy. He didn't care. He hurt. Inside and out. His shoulder was hurting like a bitch because he had refused his last painkillers. Probably a bad idea now that he thought about it, especially since Maria had insisted on driving.

"I'm not sure you would have been up to it. You know I got shot in the shoulder once and found it hard to drive for a few days."

She unlocked the door and then pushed it open. Stepping back, she took his arm to help him into the house. Like he was an invalid of some sort.

Once they were inside, she closed the door and locked it.

"Micah and Evan made sure to get your prescriptions taken care of."

"I don't need painkillers."

She said nothing, so he turned to see her giving him a wry look. "Yeah, you're a big, bad He-Man. But one of them is for infection. You want to make sure you take it."

He nodded and headed toward the couch. Damn, he was tired. Just coming home from the hospital had him feeling like a ninety-year-old man.

She was staring at him and biting on her bottom lip. Then she winced.

"Damn, I keep forgetting about that."

Rome frowned. Dammit, he thought he was over the anger, but it whipped through his blood. He held it back the best he could. He was still pissed at himself for leaving her in that position, for not picking up on Jack's issues. He was his partner, and he should have known.

Her spine stiffened, and he knew she misinterpreted it. Her boss had told him that she blamed herself for not checking Jack out, but the problem had been he wasn't officially part of the HPD anymore. They'd already started his paperwork for the resignation before Maria hit the island. He hadn't been on their list. That was Rome's fault.

"Are you sure you're alright?"

He nodded. "I'll be fine in a day or two. You heard the doctor."

She gave him an overly bright smile. "Well that's good because my flight leaves at ten tonight."

"What?" he asked, but she was already walking back to the bedroom.

"My flight. I'm going back with Agent Smith."

She didn't even slow down. She yelled it out from the room.

Anger and panic swamped him. She was leaving, just like

that. He had fucked up big time, and now he was losing her.

The hell he was.

He stood and walked as fast as he could to the bedroom. By the time he got there, he was out of breath and had to lean against the doorjamb.

"What the hell do you think you're doing?"

She looked up from zipping her bag with wide, innocent eyes. "What do you mean? I have to get back to DC."

"What about us?"

She blinked. "Us?"

"Yeah, we have a relationship here."

She chuckled, and it grated on his nerves. "The job is done. I figured you were already moving on a few days ago. You pretty much told me through your actions that you didn't want any kind of relationship with me."

"I did not."

"You did." She shrugged. "I understand. It's hard doing what we were doing and keeping the sexual feelings out of it. We both had to let off some steam."

"Steam?"

She picked up her bag and set it on the floor to roll it out. She walked to the doorway and waited for him to move.

"Maria."

"You have to move for me to get through."

He stepped aside, desperately trying to come up with something to stall her. He needed to think. When he told Micah and Evan they would be married, Rome had thought he would have time to ease himself into it.

"I didn't give you permission to leave."

She was in the kitchen. She tossed a smile over her shoulder at him. "I didn't really ask. And that part of our relationship is over, Rome. I enjoyed it, believe me. But you know how serious I am about my career."

His eyes narrowed as he studied her. "You told me you wanted to write fiction."

"I do, but I'm not about to give up a big FBI career.

Smith says I'll probably get a promotion out of this."

He watched her, and he would have never guessed what was going on in her head if he hadn't seen her fingers shake when she was putting things in her laptop case.

"Really? So you can just walk away from me, what we had?"

She nodded. "It was all part of the job."

She didn't look at him, didn't even glance in his direction. He walked up behind her. She stilled.

"Aren't you going to give me a going away kiss?"

She said nothing for a second or two. With his free hand, he brushed her hair over her shoulder, exposing her neck. He bent his head, drawing in the sweet scent of her and then placed his mouth on her pulse point. It beat wildly under his lips.

"You never struck me as a sentimental person, Rome."

She was trying to be a hardass, but her voice wavered on his name, and he knew he had her.

"I am, though. Especially when it comes to you."

"Don't." The plea almost sounded like a sob. He stepped back then turned her to face him. The tears in her eyes cut at his heart. He couldn't stand to see her in pain.

He lifted his hand and gently rubbed one tear away with his thumb. "Don't cry, baby."

"Please, don't do this to me. I'm trying to give you what you want. I can't play these kinds of games."

He would have laughed from the joy of hearing her misery over leaving him but he knew it would hurt her. He cupped her face and tilted it up to see her. God, she was a mess. Her eyes shimmered with unshed tears, and her nose was already red. He'd never seen a more beautiful sight.

"I won't as long as you promise me one thing."

She sniffed. "What?"

"Don't leave me. It'll break my heart."

Her eyes widened, and she shook her head as she tried to step away from him. He just backed her up against the table.

201

"I said don't mess with me."

"You have to give me some time to get things in order and then we can go to DC."

"What?" she squawked the question.

"I'll have to hand in my resignation and get everything in order. Plus, you have to meet my folks."

"Meet your folks?"

"I think you should meet them before we get married. And they are going to want a ceremony there, so you're just going to have to put up with that."

"What wedding?" she asked.

"Ours."

"Forgive me, but I don't know if I heard you ask the question."

"I didn't ask."

She wrestled herself away from him. "You don't want to marry me."

Her voice was now turning a little hysterical.

"What do you know about that?"

"First, I'm not going back to DC."

He frowned, confused. "But you said you were."

She drew in a breath, closing her eyes. He got the impression that she was counting backwards from ten. When she opened her eyes, she was spitting mad.

"I resigned from the FBI. There, you have it. I'm not going back there to live. Yes, to finish out all the paperwork, get rid of my apartment, then I'm moving back to Dad's place."

"That works. You can just move in here."

She shook her head. "I haven't said I was going to marry you."

"But you are."

"You don't love me. I am not going to settle for anything less ever again."

She said it with such force, he knew she was serious. He knew what she had been through as a child, what she had missed out on. Still, she was a first rate FBI agent, strong, dependable, and the sweetest woman he'd ever met. The fact that she had that hard outer shell made him love her even more.

"I do love you."

"No, you don't."

That wasn't the reaction he expected. "Yes, I do."

She was already shaking her head, and now he was getting pissed.

"I do love you. I may not like you right now, but I love you. Jesus." He shoved his hand through his hair. Women never ceased to amaze him.

"Tell me one thing that tells me you love me."

"One thing?"

Rome was still trying to come to terms with the fact that he'd told a woman he loved her for the first time in his life, and she was telling him he didn't.

"See." She brushed past him. "You don't love me. You feel guilty, or maybe you're feeling bad for acting like a jackass. I get it. Don't worry. I'm not loveable."

He caught up with her as she opened the front door. He slammed it shut, and she opened her mouth to yell at him.

"Shut up," he roared. "God, you're a pain in the ass, you know that? I tell you I love you, and you want proof. I'm willing to move to a city I detest to be with you, and you don't see it."

"I don't like your tone."

He ground his teeth as he grabbed her suitcase and tossed it across the floor. It thudded against the wall.

"Why of all the nerve—"

"I said, shut up." He started pacing. "Why do I love you? Prove it? Woman, you know how to push a man's buttons, don't you?"

She opened her mouth, and he shot her a look that had her snapping it shut.

"Don't even start comparing me to other men. Not your

father or any of your old lovers. I love you because you're strong. So strong you think you have to carry all your problems on your own. You don't ever want a helping hand."

"I'm not strong."

She whispered the comment, and he heard the shame. He stopped pacing and walked to her then. She looked so fragile at the moment he was afraid if he touched her, she would shatter.

"I'm not strong," she repeated, but louder this time. "I was so damned scared every time I was in the field. I hated it. I hate being an agent. I hate that sick rush you get when you know there's going to be trouble. Other agents get off on it, but I don't have the backbone to be an agent."

Damn her father. Damn him for making her feel that the only way she could be complete was by being an FBI agent.

"Baby, that doesn't make you weak." He did touch her then. He brushed his fingers down her arm. She seemed to collapse, the tears streaming down her face. He pulled her against him with his one good arm.

"I am. There is part of me that would be happy to live a lie and pretend you love me just to be near you. I love you so much that it's breaking me."

"You are strong." She shook her head and sniffled against his chest. "You are, baby. You are willing to walk away and try something that other people would be afraid to do. No matter what, you did a job you hated because people depended on you. That makes you a good person."

She still said nothing, so he slipped his finger under her chin.

"But despite that, despite the fact that your father tried to raise you in his image, you are your own woman. You might be tough on the outside, but you have this sweet heart. You hide it from everyone else, but I see it. I like that. From the moment I first touched you, I knew I couldn't give you up."

"Then why were you being an ass?"

"You know about what happened in Seattle?"

"The partner, she was dirty."

"I was sleeping with her. She slept with me to make sure I missed out on it. When they found Amy, I blamed myself. See, since I'd been with you, I couldn't concentrate. I figured I could put you back in the compartment."

She still didn't believe him. He could tell by the expression on her face.

"You know, a guy could get the impression you don't want to be loved by the way you're acting."

"You feel guilty."

"Yeah, for acting like an ass, and I should have picked up on Jack, but he kept it well hidden. But I'm not telling you I love you because I feel guilty. I love you because of who you are. You're tough and kind, and there is a part of you I know you've not let anyone see but me. A vulnerable part that just wants to be loved for who you are. I do love you for who you are. I want you by my side when I fall asleep, I want to breathe in your scent before I open my eyes in the morning. I want a little Maria running around the house with her mother's laugh and those gorgeous blue eyes. I can't think of being without you. I love you."

Tears were now streaming down her face. "Oh, Rome. I love you, too."

"Say it again."

"I love you. I love you." She threw herself against him, hitting his shoulder. He grunted as a twinge of pain filtered out from his shoulder.

She pulled back. "I'm sorry, Rome."

"I think this is where I'm supposed to pick you up and carry you into the bedroom."

She laughed. "How about we just walk in together?"

He stopped her. "You will marry me."

The smile she gave him reached her eyes and had his heart turning over twice. "Yes. Yes, I will."

He pulled her into the bedroom, but she tried to stop him.

"Rome, the doctor told you to take it easy."

"Okay," he said and gave her a hard tug that had her stumbling with him into the room. "I'll let you do all the hard work."

She laughed and fell on to the bed with him, the sound of it filling him with joy and lust. And love.

It was his last coherent thought for hours.

The End

ABOUT THE AUTHOR

Born to an Air Force family at an Army hospital Melissa has always been a little bit screwy. She was further warped by her years of watching Monty Python and her strange family. Her love of romance novels developed after accidentally picking up a Linda Howard book. After becoming hooked, she read close to 300 novels in one year, deciding that romance was her true calling instead of the literary short stories and suspenses she had been writing. Since her first release in 2004, Melissa has had over 30 short stories, novellas and novels released with multiple publishers in a variety of genres and time periods. Those releases include the Harmless series, a best-selling erotic romance series set in Hawaii. A Little Harmless Sex, book 1, was one of the top 100 bestselling Nook Books of 2010.

Since she was a military brat, she vowed never to marry military. Alas, fate always has her way with mortals. Her husband is an Air Force major, and together they have their own military brats, two girls, and two adopted dog daughters, and they live wherever the military sticks them. Which she is sure, will always involve heat and bugs only seen on the Animal Discovery Channel. In her spare time, she reads, complains about bugs, travels, cooks, reads some more, watches her DVD collections of Arrested Development and Seinfeld, and tries to convince her family that she truly is a delicate genius. She has yet to achieve her last goal.

You can connect with Mel all over the web:

www.melissaschroeder.net
www.twitter.com/melschroeder
www.facebook.com/melissaschroederfanpage
www.facebook.com/groups/harmlesslovers

Or email her at: Contact@MelissaSchroeder.net

recommended as any Harmless Addict will tell you, but the author takes no responsibility if a reader should become overheated. Read at your own risk.

Enjoy the following unedited excerpt:

She had been right. He had been flirting with her. That thought made most of her brain melt on the spot. When she finally gathered enough of her wits to answer, he'd moved closer, resting his hand on her car behind her. She could smell him, that musky scent of his aftershave and…Conner. It took all her control not to lean in and sniff him.

"Yeah. But then, I know just how fast to go."

His expression hardened and even in the dim light, she could see the flush on his cheeks. Knowing she was getting to him had her libido revving out of control.
"Do you know what you're messing with?"

She slipped closer. "I think that's who not what."

His mouth curved. He slid his arm around her waist pulled her close and kissed her.

At first the kiss was gentle, then he deepened it, plunging his tongue between her lips. Everything in her yearned, wanted, needed. This man had been hitting all the points for days and now, she craved him.

He moved and pressed his body against her. She would have to be dead not to feel his erection.

By the time he pulled back, her head was spinning and her heart was beating so hard, she thought she might pass out. Lord, the man was deadly with his mouth.

"Answer me one question."

She couldn't seem to open her eyes.

"Jillian, open your eyes." When she didn't respond, he snapped out, "Now."

She did as he ordered before she even thought about it.

"Were you at Rough 'n Ready for fun or was it really research for a book?"

She smiled knowing it would irritate him. She wanted to

213

push him just to see his reaction and it would do to her. "A little of both."

He didn't like that answer. She could tell by the way his eyes narrowed as he studied her. "I don't think you know what you're getting yourself into."

"Why don't you tell me about it, Conner."

She heard the challenge in her voice, knew that she was definitely hitting some hot buttons for him.

He crowded her against her car again. The heat of him surrounded her and she wanted another kiss. Another taste of the paradise she knew he would be able to offer her. Conner leaned down.

When his mouth was within a centimeter of hers, he said, "When you want to do more than play games, you let me know, Jillian."

The first Military Harmless book shot to the top of the charts and even garnered a nomination for best contemporary erotic romance from The Romance Reviews!

To prove her love and save her man, she has to go above and beyond the call of duty.

Infatuation: A Little Military Harmless Romance

Francis McKade is a man in lust. He's had a crush on his best friend's little sister for years but he has never acted on it. Besides the fact that she's Malachai's sister, he's a Seal and he learned his lesson with his ex-fiancé. Women don't like being left alone for months at a time. Still, at a wedding in Hawaii anything can happen—and does. Unfortunately, after the best night of his life, he and Mal are called away to one of their most dangerous missions.

Shannon Dupree is blown over by Kade. She's always had a crush on him and after their night together, it starts to feel a little like love. But after the mission, Kade never calls or writes, and she starts to wonder if it was all a dream. Until one night, her brother Mal drags him into her bar and grill and Shannon gets the shock of her life.

Kade isn't the man Shannon knew in Hawaii, or even the last few years. He still can't shake the terror that keeps him up at night. Worse, he is realizing that the career he loves just might be over. He isn't fit for Shannon, or the love she offers him. When she won't leave him alone, he decides to prove his point.

Shannon is still mad, but she can't help but hurt for the man she loves. He is darker, a bit more dangerous, but beneath that, he is the Kade she has known for so many years. When he pushes her to her limits in the bedroom, Shannon refuses to back down. One way or another, this military man is going to learn there is no walking away from love—not while she still has breath in her body.

Warning: This book contains two infatuated lovers, some drunken dancing, a hard-headed military man, a determined woman, some old friends, and a little taste of New Orleans. As always, ice water is suggested while reading. It might be the first military Harmless book, but the only thing that has changed is how hot our hero looks in his uniform—not to mention out of it.

Enjoy an unedited excerpt from Infatuation: A Little Harmless Military Romance:

"Are you talking about that hot Seal your brother brought with him?" May Aiona Chambers asked as she stepped up to the two women.

"Oh, May, please, could you join us in the conversation," Jocelyn said with a laugh.

"As my sister-in-law, you should be used to it by now." She dismissed Jocelyn and honed in on Shannon. "He's been watching you."

"What?"

216

"That Marine, he's been watching you all day."

Shannon snorted trying to hide the way her pulse jumped. "You're insane. Does this run in the family? You might want to adopt children, Jocelyn."

"No, really, he has. He does it when he thinks you aren't looking."

She turned around and found him easily on the other side of the dance floor. His erect posture made it easy. Even in civvies he looked like a Marine. The Hawaiian print polo shirt hugged his shoulders and was tucked neatly into the khaki dress slacks. He wasn't the tallest man in the room, but he stood out. All that hard muscle, not to mention the blond hair, and the to-die-for blue eyes made him a gorgeous package. Everything in her yearned, wanted. Of course, he wasn't looking at them. Shannon turned back to her sister and May.

"You're drinking, right?" Shannon asked.

May rolled her eyes. "No, really he has. You know what those Seals are like. He can do surveillance without you knowing. It's his job. But, you should see the way he looks at you."

She couldn't help herself. "Like how?"

"Like he wants to take a big long bite out of you."

A shiver slinked down her spine followed by a burst of heat through her blood at the thought. Since she had met him five years earlier, she had been interested in him. Kade was sexy, that was for sure, but there was something more to him than just a good-looking man. There was an innate goodness in him, one that made a woman know he would take care of her no matter what.

"If I were you, I would make use of the event to get him in bed."

Shannon snorted again, trying to keep herself from imagining it—and failing. "Please, May, tell me what you really think."

"Believe me, I know about waiting, and it isn't worth it. I

waited years for some idiot to notice me. I think of all the time we wasted dancing around like that."

"Did you just call your husband an idiot?" Jocelyn asked.

May rolled her eyes. "Evan overlooked me for years, of course he's an idiot. But, in this situation, you have to be strategic. I saw Evan almost every day. This guy, he's going to be gone again with that job of his. You have got to take advantage of the wedding and get him into bed. Get a little wedding booty."

She should be mad, but it was hard to be. May looked so innocent with her sweet smile and her voice sounded like something out of a movie. Shannon just couldn't get irritated with her. Before May could say anything else, they announced the cutting of the cake. She turned to face the banquet table and as she did, she caught Kade looking at her. It was the briefest moment, just a second, but even across all that space, she saw the heat, the longing, and felt it build inside of her. The breath backed up in her lungs. In that next instant, he looked away.

It took all her control to turn her attention back to the event at hand, seeing her brother and her sister-in-law beaming at each other, she took another sip of champagne. May was right. She had to take a chance. If he said no, if he ignored her, then she could drink herself in a stupor and have months before she had to face him.

But there was one thing Shannon Michele Dupree did right and that was being bold. She chugged the rest of her champagne, set it on the table next to her and headed off in Kade's direction. That man wouldn't know what hit him.

Now in digital everywhere, including a new Infatuation PLUS edition, which includes Harmless Shorts. Coming in print this May.

Enjoy this excerpt from new author Lexi Blake.

Sent to steal her secrets, he soon craved her submission.

The Dom Who Loved Me

Copyright 2011 Lexi Blake

A routine mission...

Sean Taggart is hunting a deadly terrorist, and his only lead is the lovely Grace Hawthorne. She's the executive assistant for an employment agency Sean suspects is a front for illegal activities. To get the truth, he is going to have to get very close to Grace, a task he is all too eager to undertake when he discovers her deliciously submissive nature.

...turns into a dangerous seduction

Soon, Grace Hawthorne is living a double life. By day, she is the widowed mother of two college- aged sons. By night, she submits to Sean's every dark desire. She's living out her wildest fantasies of pleasure—intimate acts of trust she's only read about. As passion engulfs her, a murderer strikes, and Grace learns that Sean has a deeply hidden agenda. Will Sean choose his mission and break her heart or be the Master of her dreams?

Enjoy the following excerpt for The Dom Who Loved Me:

What was he doing? He'd thought that he could charm Grace and get the information he needed, but one little encounter with her had Sean panting and thinking in the long term. He'd so much as told Grace he wanted a relationship with her. And he did. God help him, he was crazy about her. It was just one more reason to back off the intimate relationship with Grace.

Sean felt infinitely more in control as he dried off. He shut off the water and stepped into Grace's delicate, little bathroom. It was a confection of feminine frivolity. He was surprised by it since Grace always dressed so austerely. This was a little peek into her soul, like those hot shoes she wore. Sean smiled at the neatly organized bath salts and bubble bath oils she kept in an antique bin next to the clawfoot tub. There was a stack of paperbacks on the window sill. He could tell from the flowery-looking covers that Grace enjoyed lying in her tub reading romance novels. He looked through the books and quickly figured out they mostly featured BDSM. She would be very interested in what he could teach her. He looked at that tub and pictured her there.

Of course, a tub that big was really built for two.

Not going there. He didn't need to get his brain caught on the image of lying back in that tub with Grace cuddled up between his legs. He could wash her hair and then allow her to bathe him. Nope. He wasn't going there.

Sean wrapped the towel around his waist and opened the bathroom door. He'd ask Grace if maybe one of her sons had left behind something he could wear. Anything would be easier than sitting around her kitchen almost naked trying to explain that he didn't want to have sex with her when his cock so obviously did.

The sight that met him when he opened the door made him stop in his tracks. Every single thought of leaving Grace further untouched suddenly fled as his cock firmly took command.

Grace sat in the middle of her queen-sized bed. She was completely naked and on her knees. Her palms were up, lying on her thighs, and her lovely head gazed to someplace on the floor in front of her. Her eyes were submissively down, and long, auburn locks flowed around her shoulders like a silky

220

waterfall. It was the graceful position of a sub waiting for her dominant partner's command. Everything inside Sean responded to it. He'd seen submissives waiting for him in this position countless times, but his heart leapt at the sight of Grace. This wasn't some nameless sub looking for a good time. This was Grace. She'd never sat in this position for anyone else. Just for him.

"Not on the bed, Grace," he heard himself saying. "When you greet me, you do it on the
floor."

She moved quickly and found the position again. She never looked up at him, merely followed his command. Her red hair flowed freely down her back. It was wild and wavy from the humidity. It went well with her nude body, making her seem primitive and tempting. He took in every inch of her lovely, feminine form. She was petite, but curved in all the right places. Her breasts were large and natural. Her waist flowed gracefully into full hips he could grip while he fucked her. She was the most desirable woman he had ever seen. As though he hadn't just had an orgasm, his cock fought the cotton of the towel, trying to break free.

He placed a hand on her head and gave up the fight. He would regret it. He knew he would. And he also knew he couldn't walk away from her. He let the towel drop. "Your form is next to perfect. Straighten your spine a little. Those novels you've read seem to have the right idea. Look up at me."

Her chin came up. Her lovely face was placid. Those big, hazel eyes were perfectly calm, but the slight curve of her lips gave her away. She was thrilled with his response. She'd known what she was doing. His little one was going to try to top from the bottom. It would be an intricate dance between them for power. He was looking forward to many, many years of such
a struggle. This was what you didn't get from a slave, this fire and passion. She would always surprise him. Perhaps it

was time to surprise his little sub, too.

"Did you do as I asked?"

She nodded, though a little wariness entered her expression now. "I opened the wine, Sir. It's on the table."

Sure enough, she'd followed the letter of his command, but not the intent. The bottle was chilling in a little, silver bucket with two wine glasses beside it on the bedside table. "Grace, I told you I wanted to talk. Did you have any intention of talking to me?"

"Oh, yes." Her response was bouncy, as though she was happy he'd phrased it in a way she didn't have to lie about. "I think we should talk."

He would have to be more direct. He hid the smile that threatened. He was supposed to be in control. "Grace, are you trying to seduce me?"

Now her face fell, and her teeth sank into her full bottom lip. "Can I seduce you?"

He sighed. That was what this was about? Did the woman not have eyes? In the week he'd known her, he'd always had an erection around her. She was his fucking Viagra, and he'd gone way over the "erection lasting four hours" point. He didn't need a doctor. He needed her. He was far past thinking about the job. He was thinking about Grace.

And he needed to teach his little sub a lesson. "I believe you'll find you can seduce me, but first things first." He sat down on her bed. "Over my lap."

He didn't miss the hitch in her breath. It wasn't nervousness. "I won't ask again. Right now, it's a count of five. Every second you delay, I add on to
it."

Grace's gorgeous, heart-shaped ass was across his lap in no time. Her stomach pressed against his cock. She wiggled a little, trying to get situated. Sean steadied her with his left hand. "Do you know why I'm going to spank you, little one?"

"Because I was trying to manipulate you?"

222

"No, darling. I'm going to spank you because you'll like it." He brought his hand down in a short arc, the sound cracking through the silence of the room. Her skin was so pale it immediately pinkened, and her breath came out in a sweet, little squeal. She squirmed slightly. His hand came down again, on the opposite cheek. "I'll allow your sounds this time. Know that in the future, I will tie you down and gag you if you disobey me."

He planted a little slap to the center of her ass then let his fingers slip underneath to make sure he hadn't misjudged the situation. Sure enough, his Grace was sopping wet and getting more

aroused by the second. She liked her spanking. He wasn't cooling off any either, though. He could feel his cock pulsing against her heated flesh.

He shoved two fingers straight into her cunt. She was so slippery that he slid in unencumbered. He watched her back rise and fall, uneven with every jerky breath. His sweet sub was trying so hard to follow his orders. Her skin was perfectly pink and hot to the touch. She responded so well to his discipline. He would have to be careful when he used a cane or a whip on her. He couldn't wait to tie her down and put his mark on her. He pulled his fingers out and smacked her ass again two times in quick succession. He was past the point of waiting. He needed her. He lowered her down so she knelt between his legs. Her face came up. She flushed with need. Her tongue darted across those full lips of hers, and Sean's cock throbbed.

"Open."

She didn't hesitate. She opened her mouth and allowed him to thrust his aching dick between her lips. Her tongue came out to swirl around his head, making him groan. He thrust his hands into her hair. Later, he promised himself, later he would spend an evening instructing her on just how he liked his cock sucked, but for now he was overwhelmed with the need to simply use her, to know that she was his.

223

Why this woman? Why now? He couldn't lie to himself. Grace did it for him. She was smart and funny and challenging. She was so sexy that he couldn't think about her without getting hard. How had he ever thought he could play games with her and walk away?

"Wider, Grace, you can take me all the way." He held her ruthlessly, shoving his cock in and out. He peered down. The sight of his erection disappearing between her lovely lips was just about enough to undo him. When he pulled out, her cheeks hollowed as she sucked furiously trying not to lose him. Her tongue rolled over and over his turgid flesh. He let his cockhead just brush her lips before burrowing back in to that soft place at the back of her throat. One more thrust and he would spill his come down her throat. Sean's cock came out of her mouth. He wasn't coming down her throat the first time. He wanted to be buried deep in that wet pussy of hers.

"On the bed. Spread your legs." His voice was harsh even to his own ears, but Grace didn't seem to mind. She scrambled up onto her clean, quilt-covered bed, and her legs were splayed in seconds. She was gorgeously spread out for his pleasure. His fist found his cock and stroked it as he prepared to climb on the bed and claim her. He suddenly wanted to punch a wall. "Goddamn it. Grace, I have to go out to the car for something." He hadn't intended to make love to her. His condoms were in the car.

She smiled a little weakly at him and pointed to the bedside table. "I've had college boys in my house for a couple of years and no desire to become a grandmother. I made sure there were condoms in their bathrooms."

And she'd thoughtfully brought them down. She'd manipulated him, and he couldn't resist her. He reached over and grabbed one. He regarded her with his most menacing stare as he rolled the condom over his grateful cock. "I should have spanked you more."

"Later. Right now, please fuck me, Sir."

12.99   8/11/14.

LONGWOOD PUBLIC LIBRARY
800 Middle Country Road
Middle Island, NY 11953
(631) 924-6400
longwoodlibrary.org

LIBRARY HOURS

Monday-Friday	9:30 a.m. - 9:00 p.m.
Saturday	9:30 a.m. - 5:00 p.m.
Sunday (Sept-June)	1:00 p.m. - 5:00 p.m.

31665910R00142

Made in the USA
Charleston, SC
23 July 2014